D1598499

Three women
Three cups of tea
Three new beginnings

Sarah Gardner's husband went to sleep one night in November and never woke up. At forty-years-old, the new widow is left to care for their three children, all of whom are under the age of five.

Twenty-five-year-old Filipina, Kate, thought she had met the man of her dreams during what was a perfect summer vacation. Now married to the handsome American who had swept her off her feet, and over 8000 miles away from home, Kate soon realizes that her mother was right: vacations end and people change.

Louise Delaney couldn't ask for anything more. At fifty-nine, she had enjoyed almost four decades of blissful marriage to Warren—may his soul rest in peace. But Louise's seemingly perfect world is upended when she gets a visit from a sixteen-year-old who says she is Warren's daughter.

Three exceptional women—each of whose hearts are broken into a million pieces—come together in this extraordinary tale of life, love, and true friendship.

9 780995 137929

Also by the Author

The Erin O'Reilly Mysteries
Black Velvet
Irish Car Bomb
White Russian
Double Scotch
Manhattan
Black Magic
Death By Chocolate
Massacre
Flashback (coming soon)

The Clarion Chronicles
Ember of Dreams

Massacre

The Erin O'Reilly Mysteries
Book Eight

Steven Henry

Clickworks Press • Baltimore, MD

First publication: Clickworks Press, 2020
Release: CP-EOR8-INT-P.IS-1.0

Sign up for updates, deals, and exclusive sneak peeks at clickworkspress.com/join.

Ebook ISBN: 1-943383-64-1
Paperback ISBN: 978-1-943383-65-8
Hardcover ISBN: 1-943383-66-5

For my dear friend Kira, who is better than her fears and stronger than she knows.

Massacre

Combine 2 oz. tequila, 4 oz. ginger ale, ½ oz. Campari bitters in a highball glass with ice. Stir and serve.

Chapter 1

Erin O'Reilly had done dozens of interrogations, probably hundreds. She knew how to look for weak points, how to sweat a perp until he cried. She knew when to intimidate, when to bluff, when to lie, when to offer comfort and reassurance. There was nothing quite like a full confession to grease the wheels of the legal system.

But all that knowledge depended on being the one doing the interrogating. The shoe was definitely on the other foot now.

"That's enough about work, dear," Mary O'Reilly said. She carefully placed her coffee cup in the middle of its saucer and leaned forward over the table in Erin's living room. "I've been married to a police officer for forty years, and I know there's more to life than what you call 'the Job.' You must have a young man in your life somewhere."

"Don't you ever give up, Mom?" Erin said, stalling for time.

Mary clasped her hands on her knee like the kindest, warmest-hearted, most persistent interrogator in the history of policing. "You know we don't give up in this family."

"I really am pretty busy with work," Erin said. She couldn't lie to her mother. Every time she tried, the O'Reilly matriarch saw right through her. But she absolutely did not want to tell her mom about Morton Carlyle. For starters, Mary would think he was too old for her. But that was a minor detail compared with her family's history with him. If Mary told Erin's dad about Carlyle, Sean O'Reilly just might crack open his rifle case and come out of retirement long enough to blow a few holes in him. Sean knew Carlyle from his own days on the Job, and wouldn't trust him with the time of day, let alone his only daughter. Thank goodness, Sean was visiting Erin's brother and sister-in-law this afternoon. He was even better at seeing through Erin than her mom was.

"You really could have tried to make something work with that nice art dealer," Mary went on relentlessly.

"I told you, Mom, he was the one who broke it off," Erin said. "He couldn't handle dating a cop."

"It's really not so hard, once you get used to it," Mary said.

"You can get used to anything," Erin retorted. "A few more gunfights, I'll get used to people shooting at me."

"Don't say that, dear," Mary said with a shudder. "We do worry about you."

"Then you see the problem," Erin said. "It's a tough gig."

"So you haven't been seeing anyone?" Mary pressed.

And Erin hesitated. She knew it the moment it happened, and she cursed herself for it, but she just couldn't help it. Even as she opened her mouth to try to deflect, to change the subject, to say *anything*, she saw the spark of triumph in her mother's eyes and knew she was screwed.

"It's... complicated," she said weakly. "It's not like I'm going to be bringing him to meet the parents anytime soon."

"I understand, dear," Mary said. "But remember, your clock is running. If you want children, you can't wait forever."

"How many grandkids do you want?" Erin couldn't resist asking. "You've got Patrick and Anna already. And it's not exactly easy to run down perps if I can't see my shoes."

"I don't know how you young people balance a career and a family," Mary admitted. "It really was easier for my generation."

"I'd have gone crazy sitting around the house all day," Erin said.

"It's busier than you think," Mary objected. "And more rewarding. Erin, the first time I saw your little face staring up at me..." She smiled, remembering the moment. Then she shook herself back into the present. "But all in good time, dear. First, you need to find the right man. Is this young fellow the right one for you?"

"I..." Erin began, having no idea how she was going to finish her sentence.

Her phone saved her, buzzing to life in her pocket. She pulled it out and saw the name of her commanding officer.

"Sorry, Mom, it's work," she said, trying to hide her relief. She thumbed the screen. "O'Reilly."

"You awake?" Lieutenant Webb asked. "And sober?"

"Sir, it's three o' clock," she said. "I know it's my day off, but seriously, who do you think I am?"

"Neshenko could be drunk already," Webb said.

"That's a good point," Erin admitted. "What's up?"

"Sorry to bother you on your down day," Webb said. "But you know the drill. You're only really off-duty when you're dead. Something big just went down. A restaurant's on fire."

Erin was perplexed. "We're investigators, not first responders, sir."

Webb sighed. "I know what we are, O'Reilly. FDNY's already on scene. But most fires don't start with Molotov cocktails and machine-guns."

"Machine-guns?" Erin echoed.

"And that makes it a Major Crimes problem," Webb said. "This looks like a multiple homicide. Get to 160 Mulberry, Little

Italy. And wear something you don't care about. It's going to be a dirty one."

Erin stood up. "Sorry, Mom," she said again. "Duty calls."

Her partner Rolf, always keyed to her mood, sprang to his feet, tail wagging. He didn't understand the meaning of the term "day off."

"I remember how that goes," Mary said, getting to her feet. "Well, it's been a nice visit anyway, dear. I'll just pop over to Junior's house with your father, Shelley, and the children. I hope you have time for a hug before you run off to save the world."

"Always," Erin said. She wasn't a very huggy person as a rule, but she'd have needed a heart of stone not to want one from Mary O'Reilly. The woman put all the warmth and comfort of home into every embrace.

Thus fortified, Erin quickly changed into some of her older clothes, as Webb had advised, and set off for Little Italy. Rolf bounded into his compartment in the back of her unmarked Charger. She put the car in gear and rolled out.

* * *

Erin saw the smoke from three blocks away, rising over lower Manhattan. As she got closer, she was able to follow the flashing lights of squad cars, fire engines, and ambulances. The street was choked with emergency vehicles. Lights, sirens, and blaring horns overwhelmed her senses. Poor Rolf, with his sensitive ears, was having an even worse time.

Erin parked as close to the scene as she could. She got Rolf and dismounted, making her way toward the billowing smoke. She didn't see Lieutenant Webb, but she noticed the Bomb Squad van in front of the building and angled that way. A young guy with a military buzz cut was standing next to the van, talking to an engine captain from the Fire Department.

"Hey, Skip!" she called, recognizing the explosives guy.

"Hey, Erin!" Skip Taylor replied. "You might want to keep back a little. Fire's still going."

"I can see that," she said. She turned to the firefighter. "Sir, what's the situation?"

"Firebombing," the captain said. He pointed to the front of the building. Dense clouds of smoke poured through the shattered plate glass. "Excuse me, Detective. I know you have your job to do, but right now, I have mine. We're containing the blaze. I've got Engine 24's crew working the fire, and 55 doing a rescue search."

"They're inside?" Erin asked, appalled. She'd made entry to burning buildings back when she'd been working Patrol, but it was never safe or easy. The fire in front of her was much worse than any she'd dared approach.

"Yes, ma'am," he said. "Excuse me." He turned and went quickly toward the fire.

"What can you tell me, Skip?" Erin asked the bomb tech.

"I was just talking to the cap about the danger of secondaries."

"Secondaries?"

"Secondary explosions," he explained. "We've shut down the gas lines, and I'm guessing they don't have propane tanks inside, so the worst I'd expect would be a grease fire, but the kitchen's gonna be dangerous."

"O'Reilly!"

Lieutenant Webb hurried over, Vic Neshenko looming behind him. Erin's commanding officer had his trademark unlit cigarette in one hand. Webb looked unhappy, even by his standards.

Vic, on the other hand, was cheerful. He always got energized by action. "Welcome to the party," he said.

"What've we got?" she asked.

"Dispatch got a 10-10S," Webb said, the code for a crime in progress with shots fired. "We had a Patrol unit less than a block away. When they rolled up, they took fire from at least two automatic weapons, so they fell back and called for backup."

"Any officers hit?" Erin asked sharply.

"Nope," Vic said. "Lucky bastards. Got some holes punched in their car."

Erin suppressed a shiver, remembering a similar situation she'd been in last year. "Glad they're okay," she said.

"While they were pinned down, some joker tossed a Molotov through the storefront," Webb continued. "Then the perps took off around the corner. They must've had a car waiting. Backup arrived in less than two minutes, but the shooters were already gone."

"Traffic cams?" Erin asked.

"No good," Vic said. "We'll check 'em, but there's a lot of traffic on that road, and we don't have footage in the middle of the block, so we don't know which car was theirs. We may be able to ID the shooters at the corner, but we'll have to run all the plates on all the cars."

"And theirs will be stolen," Erin predicted. "They've probably already dumped the car."

"Probably," Webb gloomily agreed.

"How many shooters?" she asked.

"The uniforms saw three," Vic said.

"We've got spent brass all over the sidewalk," Webb said, indicating the front of the building. "Of course, New York's Bravest are contaminating the hell out of the crime scene as we speak. I hate arson jobs."

"On the bright side," Vic said, "the shooting ended before we got here."

"You're in a good mood," Erin observed.

"Can't a guy be happy?"

"Not if it's you," she said. "I'd call that highly suspicious. I only see you happy when you're in a fight."

"You gotta watch out, Erin," he said. "All this time around crooks and psychos is making you paranoid."

"It's not paranoia..." she began.

"...if they're out to get you," he finished. "Hey, Lieutenant, how long you think they're gonna take hosing down our crime scene?"

"Depends on what they find," Webb said. He was starting to say something else when a distinctive sound cut through the controlled chaos on the street. A series of loud pops, it was immediately recognizable to anyone who knew it.

Erin and Vic had their sidearms drawn before they'd even fully registered what they'd heard. Skip, who'd served in combat in Iraq, was even faster. He was crouching behind his van's engine block by the time Erin shouted, "Shots fired!"

"Where the hell did that come from?" Webb demanded, drawing his old service revolver. Cops and firefighters were scattering, taking cover and looking frantically for the shooter. More shots rang out.

"Over there!" Vic shouted, pointing at the burning building.

"You've got to be kidding," Erin muttered.

The fire captain ran toward Webb, a radio at his ear. "Lieutenant!" he shouted. "I've got men inside taking fire! I have a man down! I need cover!"

"Get me masks and fire gear," Webb snapped. He waved over the nearest Patrol officers. "I need some volunteers. We've got men in there who need help."

There was the briefest hesitation. Then a young officer whose nametag read RUIZ stepped forward. "I'll go, sir."

"I'm in," Vic growled. Two more shots came from the building. Everyone but Vic flinched.

"Let's do it," Erin said. Turning to the captain, she quickly asked, "Is the fire safe for my K-9?"

"Can he do SAR?" the captain replied, referring to Search and Rescue training.

"Yeah."

"Then we need him. Let's move!"

The police grabbed firefighter overcoats and oxygen tanks on their way. Erin was trying not to worry about Rolf. He was absolutely willing to go, and being low to the ground, he wouldn't have as much to fear from smoke inhalation as the rest of them, but he wouldn't be able to stay inside long. And he couldn't wear an oxygen mask without compromising his sense of smell.

"*Komm,*" she ordered, giving the command in Rolf's native German. He trotted beside her, alert and attentive.

"You better stay outside, sir," Erin told Webb. He tended to get short of breath at the best of times, what with his smoking habit and extra bulk.

"You giving me orders, O'Reilly?" he retorted. "I've been sucking smoke since I was sixteen. I'm used to it."

Ruiz looked very young, and very scared, but he buckled on his gear with steady hands. The four officers formed up outside. Even through the protective gear, Erin could feel the heat of the fire, like an open oven door.

"Let's go," Webb ordered.

"NYPD!" Erin shouted as they plunged in. "Sound off, guys! Where are you?"

The fire made a strange, hollow roaring sound. Everything was smoke, heat, and flickering flame. Erin heard the rasp of her own breathing in the oxygen mask. The smoke was disorienting. Even though they were barely inside, she had trouble remembering the way out. Strange shapes of tables and chairs appeared and disappeared through the smoke. If anyone answered her call, she didn't hear them.

"Rolf!" she ordered. "*Such!*"

Hearing his "search" command, the K-9 moved forward, sliding with his belly close to the floor. How he could smell anything but smoke was a mystery, but he was clearly on the scent of someone. Erin held his leash in one hand, her Glock nine-millimeter in the other. She was in the lead, the other officers keeping close so as not to lose contact.

Rolf suddenly stopped and scratched the floor. Erin saw a body at her feet. She knelt and saw it was a man, dressed in street clothes, face down. Blood was pooled around him. He didn't seem to be breathing, but it was hard to tell.

"Got a casualty!" she shouted. Even as she said it, a sustained burst of gunfire came from very close at hand.

"Christ!" Vic said. He snapped off two shots in return.

"Don't fire blind!" Webb barked. "You out there! This is the NYPD! Put down the weapon and give up! Otherwise you're going to die in here! We're here to help you, idiot!"

"Fire Department!" someone shouted to Erin's left. "We got a man down!"

"Rolf!" Erin repeated. "*Such!*" She nudged him in the direction of the voice.

Rolf was off again, sneezing and snorting. Erin went with him, keeping as low as she could. Another gunshot sounded, followed by two more from Vic.

"God damn it, Neshenko!" Webb shouted. "Cease fire!"

Erin found an overturned table, a looming shape in the smoke. Behind it, three firefighters were huddled with a fourth one at their feet. The wounded man was writhing in pain.

"We'll cover you!" Erin shouted.

Ruiz was behind her. He tapped her shoulder to let her know he was there. He rested the barrel of his pistol on the edge of the upturned table. "Go!" he said.

Erin and Rolf moved back the way they'd come. The firefighters followed, carrying their downed buddy. No more shots were fired. Erin dared to hope Vic might've gotten lucky. Or maybe the shooter had gone down from smoke inhalation, or suffered an outbreak of common sense and just stopped shooting.

The police and firefighters tumbled out of the building onto the sidewalk, into blessed fresh air and sunlight. Erin thought a bleak, cold March day had never felt so good. They pulled off their masks and sucked in the air. Rolf, at her side, gave a wheezing cough and sank to the pavement.

Erin dropped to one knee beside her dog. "Good boy," she said. "*Sei brav*, Rolf. *Sei brav*."

He wagged his tail and coughed again.

"I need some help here!" she shouted. "It's my K-9!"

One of the firemen hurried over, holding a special oxygen mask. Erin thanked God for Americans' love for their pets. The FDNY had taken to stocking masks for dogs and cats in their trucks, and Rolf was the beneficiary of the policy. He was soon breathing more easily, but Erin stayed beside him, like a good partner should.

After the shooting, the firefighters drew back from the building and concentrated on containment, keeping the fire from spreading. There wasn't much left to save in the restaurant by now anyway, and they weren't about to risk more lives over a big pile of wet ashes. The uniformed officers on scene, very twitchy, kept an eye on the blaze and fingered their weapons.

Erin's colleagues were a short distance away. Webb had his hands on his hips and was looking up at Vic, who had six inches of height and many pounds of muscle on his boss.

"Detective Neshenko," Webb said in a dangerously quiet voice.

"Sir," Vic said, looking at a point just over his commander's shoulder.

"I'd love to hear why you disobeyed a direct order."

"Incoming fire outranks the whole chain of command, sir."

"You could've killed someone."

"I think I did kill someone."

"There's easier ways to get time off than going on modified assignment," Webb growled.

"We had a man down," Vic said. "If we weren't supposed to shoot back, why'd the department issue us guns?"

"You've already earned an insubordination rip for this," Webb said. "Want to try for two?"

Vic didn't say anything. His cheek twitched slightly.

Rolf nosed at Erin's hand. She stroked his shoulder. The important thing was that they were okay. The fireman who'd been shot had been hit in the calf. It didn't look like a serious injury. She understood Webb's anger. With all that smoke in the place, Vic couldn't possibly have known what was around his target. He could've easily hit an innocent victim. Hell, maybe he had; they wouldn't know until the fire died down.

Erin settled herself to wait, resting a hand on her K-9. The smell of smoke wafted up from the Shepherd's fur to her nostrils. Rolf had already had a tough day, and now he had a bath to look forward to.

"Lieutenant!"

A uniformed officer was running around the corner. He looked agitated, which wasn't surprising, considering they were at an unsecured crime scene where shots had been fired and which was still ablaze.

Webb turned to the man. "What is it?"

"We've got bodies, sir."

Webb looked confused. Erin felt the same. This guy's uniform was clean. He hadn't been inside the burning building. What could he possibly have to report?

"You looked in there?" Webb asked.

"Not inside," the officer replied. "Around back. By the service door. Three of 'em. All dead."

"You sure?"

"Yeah, I counted."

Webb gave him a look of long-suffering patience. "I mean, are you sure they're dead?"

"Yes, sir."

"I guess we'd better take a look," Webb said. "Neshenko? Can I count on you not to shoot anyone else?"

"As long as they don't shoot at me," Vic said.

"O'Reilly? Your K-9 okay?"

Erin looked at her dog. "How you doing, kiddo? You ready to go back to work?"

Rolf wriggled his body to get his feet under him. He kicked at the oxygen mask on his face as if he was scratching an itch.

Erin knew he wasn't badly damaged. He wasn't coughing or wheezing anymore, and while his eyes were streaming, they didn't look too bloodshot. Rolf would be more bothered by being left out of the action than he would be by any physical inconvenience.

"Okay, boy," she said, helping him out of the mask. "*Komm.*"

Three detectives and one K-9 followed the uniform around to the back alley.

"I thought all the shooters were out front," Vic said.

"That was my understanding," Webb said.

"Maybe they got hit inside," Erin suggested, "and crawled out to die, trying to get away from the flames."

"All three?" Vic wondered. "Seems unlikely. Whoa."

They'd just rounded the corner and seen the bodies, laid out as promised.

"Now there's something you don't see every day," Webb said.

Erin nodded. She'd been at plenty of shooting scenes. Street violence, as a rule, was messy. Even trained shooters tended to fire wildly when the chips were down. Erin knew the numbers. On the firing range, cops could nail their targets over ninety percent of the time. But in gunfights, they hit with about one in six bullets. Untrained street thugs did worse. The victims in a gangland shootout tended to have holes in any number of random body parts, and getting killed in that kind of fight was more about bad luck than enemy skill.

This was different. The three bodies were sprawled just outside the restaurant's back door, with pools of blood around each man's head. They'd all gone down to perfect headshots.

"Bang, bang, bang," Vic said quietly. "That's some damn good shooting."

"Steady hands," Webb agreed. He approached the first body and knelt beside it, peering at the bullet hole in the man's forehead. "One shot each. We'll need to get Levine to take a look at these, but I'm not seeing any powder tattooing."

"Not close enough for execution-style," Erin said. "Besides, looks like two of these guys were shot from the front." Even coldblooded killers tended to murder people from behind. Killing a man was hard enough even if you didn't have to looking him in the eye.

"Looks like this guy took one in the temple," Vic said, pointing to another victim. "I'm guessing he was the first one to get hit. That must've gotten the attention of the other two. They turned toward the shooter and he snuffed 'em, one, two."

"Fast shooting," Erin said. "Fast and accurate." She was looking at the dead guys' hands. One of them was holding a pistol, a small revolver. The other's hands were empty, but he had an automatic stuffed in his waistband. She crouched and peered at the revolver, seeing the blunt tips of bullets in every cylinder.

"They never got the chance to shoot back," she said. "One poor sap didn't even get his weapon out."

"Must've been more than one shooter," Vic said. "No one's that fast and good."

"Either that, or we've got a trained sniper," Webb said. He didn't sound happy about it.

"Whichever it is," Vic said, "this is more than a homicide."

"Yeah," Erin agreed. "It's a war."

Chapter 2

Erin and her colleagues had to wait for the fire to die down before they could work the full crime scene. In the meantime, they had the three bodies in the back alley, but they needed to wait on Sarah Levine, the medical examiner, before they could do much with them.

"I should've brought a deck of cards," Vic muttered.

"At least there aren't any windows in back of the building," Erin said. "The fire won't get at these poor bastards."

Webb was still crouched over the bodies, scanning them carefully. "These guys are Italians," he said.

"Well, yeah," Vic said. "We are in Little Italy. That's not exactly unusual."

"Two young men, one older one," Webb continued. "And if you're right, Neshenko, the old guy got it first."

"And the two younger ones were carrying guns," Erin said. "Bodyguards?"

Webb nodded. "That means the old man was the target. I don't see a piece on him. He's the least dangerous of the bunch. Why shoot him first, unless killing him was the point?"

"But if it was a sniper," Erin said, "why bother shooting the other two at all? Why not just take the one shot and get away?"

"Targets of opportunity?" Vic guessed. "Or maybe we've got a sick son of a bitch who just likes killing people."

Webb pulled a pencil out of his trench coat and probed at the entrance wound in one of the younger guys' heads. "Levine can confirm," he said. "But this looks like a nine-millimeter hole. Maybe a .38."

"Not a rifle, then," Erin said.

"Handgun," Webb agreed.

"Please stop poking my body," a woman said from behind them.

Vic choked on whatever he'd been about to say. He leaned against the wall and recovered his breath, while the other two turned to see Doctor Levine approaching.

"Hey," Erin said, wondering if the other woman had any idea how odd her word choice was. "We've got three out here, at least one more inside. Probably more."

"GSWs," Webb added.

Levine went directly to the first body, without saying anything else to the detectives. She was already wearing her gloves. She examined the dead man for several moments.

"Cause of death is obvious," she said, not directing her comments to anyone in particular. Levine tended to talk to herself. "Cerebral hemorrhage as a result of a single gunshot wound to the cranium. The exit wound indicates the bullet will be somewhere downrange. The wound channel transects the left frontal and parietal lobes, exiting just above the occipital. Death was instantaneous."

"We're thinking handgun," Webb said.

"The caliber supports your hypothesis," Levine said, keeping her eyes on the victim. "Lack of powder stippling indicates the range was at least thirty centimeters."

"Assuming the bodies haven't been moved, the shooter was

on this line," Webb said, pacing the alley away from the body.

"If we're thinking one shooter, he wouldn't have had time to move more than a step or two," Erin said, checking the angles. She knew stationary shooting was much easier than firing on the go. "If he shot all three from the same spot, it would've been about here." She toed the pavement.

"The second victim presents almost identically to the first," Levine said. "Cause of death is congruent."

"If it was a nine-mil, it was an automatic," Vic said. "That means we should have casings. The bad guys didn't have time to recover their brass."

Erin nodded. While Levine continued her examination, they canvassed the alley. Unfortunately, shell casings didn't tend to lie in nice, neat piles. Once ejected from a gun, they could fly surprising distances. Even knowing where the shooter had likely been standing, it still took a few minutes of looking through the litter in the alley before Vic snapped his fingers.

"Got one!" he announced. "It's a nine, all right."

"Most common ammunition in America," Webb sighed. "At least we'll be able to match it with the weapon, assuming we can recover it."

No one commented that the killer would have to be awfully careless to let that happen. All of them could see this was a professional job, and professional hitmen knew to get rid of a murder weapon as soon as possible.

Erin found another casing, and Rolf nosed out a third with his keen snout for gunpowder. They marked the spent brass with yellow evidence numbers and left them for the CSU guys to pick up and bag. Then Erin stood next to her boss and watched Levine work.

"This is a weird one," she said.

Webb nodded. "I can see the guys shooting up the place and throwing in firebombs. That's typical gangland MO. A little heavy-handed, maybe, but typical. But then we've got this professional operator waiting out back? Why have your best shooter on the bench? They should've been out front."

"I think the plan was to flush the target out the back," Erin said. "It's like they do in England when they hunt birds."

"Yeah," Vic said, joining them. "Those upper-class idiots get all their people to beat the bushes while they wait with the guns. Then, when the pheasants or grouse or whatever try to get away from the beaters, the shooters gun 'em down."

"What do you know about English aristocrats?" Webb asked, surprised.

"Not much," Vic said. "But I know a lot about shotguns. You oughta try trap-shooting sometime. Might improve your marksmanship."

"This is not a good time to discuss shooting with me," Webb said dryly.

Vic's jaw tightened and he shut up.

"It's a good thought, though," Webb said. "I think O'Reilly might be right."

"This guy was someone important," Erin guessed. "Mafia, maybe?"

"We'll know soon enough," Webb replied. "CSU should be able to get us IDs on the ones outside, at least."

"We'll need dental records for the poor mopes in the fire," Vic added.

"And that needs to wait for the fire to be out," Webb sighed. "We'd better get comfortable."

*   *   *

As they stood back and watched the building burn, Skip Taylor wandered over. Like them, the bomb tech didn't have much to do for the moment. His job would come later, identifying the incendiary devices used to start the fire.

"Good shooting, Tex," he said to Vic.

"How do you know?" Vic retorted.

"Your Tango's down," Skip said, using a slang term from his military days meaning "target."

"Maybe the fire got him," Erin said.

"Oh, the fire definitely got him," Skip said, grinning.

"What do you mean?" she asked.

"Saw it happen all the time in Baghdad. There's a roadside bomb, or a gas tank gets lit up, some dope goes down in the fire, and a few minutes later the dead guy's ammo starts popping off."

"Damn it," Vic said. "I should've known. That guy wasn't shooting at me."

"Nope," Skip agreed. "His bullets were cooking off from the heat. He was done before you even showed up."

"Congratulations," Erin said to Vic. "You just won a gunfight with a dead man."

"You think this is funny?" he growled.

"A little bit."

Vic shook his head. "This is another thing I'm never gonna live down."

*   *   *

It took about four hours of what the firefighters called "surround and drown" until smoke stopped pouring out of the charred remains of the restaurant. By that time, debris from the fire had clogged the storm drains and water from the hoses had pretty much flooded the street. It was March, and the cold seeped up into Erin's body through her wet shoes. She'd loaded Rolf back into her car, and wished she'd done the same for herself. She tried not to shiver. Vic, doing his stoic Russian bit, gave no sign of discomfort. Webb was working his way through his second pack of cigarettes.

In the meantime, they had one useful witness. A kid, Tim Oney, sixteen years old, claimed to have seen the whole thing. He was more excited than traumatized, unable to hold still. Webb asked the questions, while Erin and Vic listened.

"What happened?"

"We had early dismissal today from my school, so they let us out at 1:30."

"What school?"

"Bard High School, over on Houston Street. I picked up some snacks on the way home. I was gonna get together with a couple buddies and play Call of Duty until Mom kicks them out. I got Mountain Dew, a box of Twinkies, and some chips. Is that important?"

"Anything you remember might be important. We'll decide that. Just tell us what you saw."

"Anyway, I was walking past Antonio's when I saw these three guys. They were wearing long black coats. They walked up to the windows and pulled out guns from under their coats, just like in the movies. You know, like the lobby scene in The Matrix? It looked like that. You know, when Neo opens up his coat and he's got all these guns, and..."

"Kid, I've seen it."

"Oh, yeah. Sure. Well, it was like that, except they only had one gun each, at least that I saw. Maybe they had more under their coats. But they hauled out what looked like an AR-15, an SA80, and a Benelli M4."

"You recognized the guns?" Vic broke in.

"I play a lot of FPS."

"FPS?" Webb asked.

"First-person shooters, you know, Call of Duty, Counterstrike, Halo."

"Okay, kid. That's good. That's the sort of details we need.

Are you sure about the guns?"

"Yeah. Well, the SA80 and the AR-15 for sure. I'm pretty sure the shotgun was a Benelli. It had a pistol grip."

"What happened then?"

"They just started shooting, right through the windows. And it was loud. I mean, seriously loud. I think they tone down the noise in games. It was scary, but kind of cool, too, you know? Like, there's this action scene happening right in front of me. I should've got my phone out and taken a picture, or some video, but it was so fast, you know?

"Anyway, they shot the shit out of the windows, and people were screaming and running around outside. I guess they were screaming inside, too. Then some cops showed up and yelled something, and the guys with the rifles shot at the cops. But they didn't hit any of them. Then the guy with the shotgun took out a Molotov cocktail, you know, a bottle full of gas, and he threw it inside. The weird thing was, he didn't light it first. You know, in the movies they always have a rag sticking out the top that they light with a lighter? But this one wasn't lit. But that didn't matter, because as soon as it hit inside, it blew up. It was a big frickin' fireball, man. It's a good thing for those guys that the windows were already shot out, or the glass would've cut them all up. I could feel the heat all the way from the other side of the street."

"You're sure the bottle wasn't already on fire when it went inside?" Erin asked.

"Yeah. Maybe he threw it into the kitchen and hit the stove? It would've been a hell of a good throw. I think maybe it had something that wasn't just gasoline in it, maybe something that went off when the bottle broke and the air hit it? I'm gonna ask Mr. Reynolds, my chem teacher. He knows a lot about chemical reactions and stuff."

"What happened then?"

"The two guys with the rifles kept shooting to keep the cops pinned down. Then they took off running around that corner."

"Did you see their faces?"

"Yeah, but they were wearing hats and sunglasses, and they had the collars on their coats pulled way up, so I didn't see much."

"Were they white? Black? Middle Eastern? Italian?"

"They were white guys, I think. They had on gloves along with the masks, so it was hard to tell. But yeah, they were white. At least, one of them was. I saw his neck over the top of his coat."

"What else can you tell me about them?"

"They had nice shoes."

"Nice shoes?"

"Like, the kind of shoes guys wear if they work in an office. Not like sneakers, you know? Black shoes, black pants, black coats, black hats."

"Kid's a good witness," Erin said, once they'd let Tim go.

"Plays too many video games," Webb said. "I'm glad I have daughters. But yeah, he caught a lot of details. It definitely sounds like a professional hit. But he didn't see the fourth shooter."

"He wouldn't have," she said. "The fourth guy was around back the whole time."

Finally, the fire captain announced the fire was out and the site was secure. The CSU team moved in to start sorting out the bodies from the rest of the burnt-out rubble. The meat wagon had arrived in the meantime, driven by those two guys from the city morgue, Hank and Ernie.

"Jesus, not them again," Vic muttered.

"You think they volunteer for the bad homicides?" Erin wondered aloud.

"Wouldn't surprise me."

Hank jerked a thumb toward the back alley. "You want the brainless wonders or the barbecue?"

"Let's save the leftovers," Ernie said. "They gotta take pictures first. Meantime, I'm gonna live la vida loca."

Hank raised an eyebrow.

"*C'mon, man, Ricky Martin?*" Ernie prompted. Then he sang, "She'll make you take your clothes off and go dancing in the rain. She'll make you live her crazy life, but she'll take away your pain... like a bullet to your brain!"

Hank nodded and joined in on the chorus. "Upside, inside out, she's livin' la vida loca!"

The two of them salsa-danced into the back alley and out of view, still singing.

Vic exchanged a look with Erin. "I know the Lieutenant's pissed about me letting off rounds," he said. "But do you really think he'd mind if I kneecapped those two?"

She shrugged. "He might even help you fill out the paperwork."

The detectives picked over the wreckage along with the CSU guys, but it was hard to figure what had happened. It was one of the messiest crime scenes Erin had ever seen; at least, the restaurant was. The back alley was almost too clean.

"This is weird," Erin said for the second time that day. "It's like two different crimes stacked on top of each other."

"Say that again," Webb said.

"What?"

"Two different scenes." The Lieutenant spun an unlit cigarette in his fingers. "These MOs don't match at all."

"No," Erin agreed. "You think the shooter in the back alley wasn't connected with the firebombers?"

Vic shrugged. "Or it's like we thought before, and the whole thing was a plan to drive them out the back."

"Maybe we're looking for two gangs," Webb said thoughtfully.

"Or one gang and a lone wolf," Erin said.

"If the shooter out back was a loner, he's one hell of a confident guy," Vic said. "One man with a handgun hitting a whole team of Mafia goons?"

"This is speculation," Webb said. "And we don't have enough facts to start making guesses."

"I thought guesses were for when we didn't have facts," Vic objected.

"And that's why you're still a Detective Third Grade and I'm a Lieutenant," Webb said.

Vic bristled.

"He means we need to make educated guesses," Erin said. "Not wild ones."

"I know what he meant," Vic growled. "But even when he's right, he's kind of an—"

"Thin ice, Neshenko," Webb said, pointing the cigarette at him like the barrel of a gun.

"—astronomical pain," Vic caught himself, then added, "sir."

"We're done here, for now," Webb said. "You missed the witness statements, O'Reilly. But there wasn't much to them. We'll go back to the precinct, check the traffic cams, go over the statements again, and wait for IDs on our victims."

"Mafia," Vic predicted. "This is a big batch of misdemeanor homicides, bad guys taking out other bad guys. My prediction is, we'll find out some jackasses did the world a favor."

"What about the rest of the people in the restaurant?" Erin asked. "We've probably got civilians in there, too."

That shut Vic up.

* * *

Erin called her brother's house from the car. Her sister-in-law Michelle answered the phone.

"Hello?"

"Hey, Shelley," Erin said.

"Erin! We're just about to set the table. We can hold dinner for you if you hurry."

"Sorry, I can't. That's why I'm calling. I've got a work thing. Mom and Dad will understand."

"So do I," Michelle said. Her husband was a trauma surgeon, and she was no stranger to unusual hours and last-minute cancellations. "I'll tell them. Anna was looking forward to seeing Rolf, though. You have to bring him by sometime soon."

"You ever think about getting a dog?"

Michelle laughed. "Don't let Anna hear you say that. She's already leaning on me." Then she lowered her voice. "Speaking of family pressure, your mom's been pumping me for information about your boyfriend."

"Oh, God." Erin wanted to put a hand over her face. Michelle was the only member of Erin's family who knew about Carlyle. Shelley didn't know his name; Erin wasn't crazy enough to spill that. But she did know Erin was seeing a guy with a criminal record, one who'd been involved in one of her previous cases. That by itself might be enough for her dad to crack the whole thing open. Erin often suspected the only reason Sean O'Reilly hadn't made Detective was that he'd preferred to keep doing Patrol work. He was plenty smart, with great street instincts and a career's worth of experience.

"Erin? You okay?"

"Yeah. What did you tell her?"

"Nothing!" Michelle sounded shocked. "You're my sister. I would never!"

Erin smiled. "Thanks, Shelley."

"But you should tell them. I mean, it's good news, isn't it?

Mary's been itching for you to find the right guy for years now, and I know you're crazy about him."

"That obvious?"

"That obvious."

"It's complicated," Erin said. "Look, just sit on this for me, okay? I owe you."

"Copy that," Michelle said and giggled. "That's what you say, right?"

"That's what we say," Erin confirmed. "I'll come by when I can, but if it's late, I'll drop you a text instead. I don't want to wake up the kids, and I don't know how long I'll be stuck on duty."

"Okay, Erin. Take care."

*   *   *

Information was already flowing through the pipeline by the time Erin, Vic, and Webb got to the Precinct 8 station. They had a statement from the main witness, recorded from an officer's body camera, and preliminary IDs on the three victims from the alley based on documents in their pockets. They also had snapshots from CSU waiting on their computers.

"Neshenko, plug these guys into facial recognition," Webb said.

Vic got to work on the computer. It always amazed Erin how fast the NYPD's software could get results. Just a few minutes later, he had their answer.

"Sal Pietro, Nick Carmine, and Marco Conti," he said. "We'll do the prints to make sure, but it's them. They've all got records. Mafia, like I said. Pietro and Carmine were muscle, Conti was a mid-level associate."

"Which family?" Webb asked.

"Lucarelli."

Erin felt a shiver. She'd tangled with some of the Lucarellis on their last big case, and it hadn't been pleasant. "These guys have any connection to Vinnie the Oil Man?"

"Of course," Vic said, giving her a funny look. "I said they were Lucarellis. Vincenzo Moreno runs the family these days."

"How nice," Webb said dryly. "I was wondering how long it'd take the Oil Man to cross our path again. He'll make it nice and slippery, I expect."

"I don't suppose he's one of the stiffs in the restaurant," Erin said without much hope.

"We're not that lucky," Vic said. "Do we want to talk to him?"

"Wrong question," Webb said. "I think we'd all be happy never to see him again. But we may have to lean on him a little. Not that it'll do any good. He won't tell us a thing. Probably best to leave him out of it."

"So it's definitely a mob hit," Erin said. "Who's got a bone to pick with the Lucarellis? What side of the business was Conti in?"

"Narcotics," Vic said. "He did some time for possession, but that was a long time ago. Nowadays I don't think he was actually touching the product."

"This wasn't a drug rip anyway," Webb said. "The shooters didn't steal anything."

"That we know of," Erin put in. "Maybe the guys in back had something and the fourth shooter got it."

"Okay," Webb said. "Let's get in with our underworld contacts. Find out who's on the outs with the Lucarellis."

"I'll talk to Narcotics," Vic said. "See if they've got anything."

Erin knew where this was going. "I've got a couple guys I can talk to," she said. "Maybe they know something."

Somehow, she always came back to the Irish Mob.

Chapter 3

The closest bar to Erin's apartment was the Barley Corner. She'd inherited her father's fondness for good whiskey, and the Corner stocked the very best. As an added incentive, her drinks there were on the house, ever since she'd saved the pub, and its owner, from being blown apart. On top of that was the fact that the owner, Morton Carlyle, was her boyfriend. And right now, he was one of her best sources into what might have sparked the vicious mob hit.

The Corner was always full of Irish wiseguys, which was awkward. But most of those who knew about her were under the impression she was Carlyle's insider with the NYPD. It pissed her off that anyone would think she was dirty, but it was a necessary deception to preserve Carlyle's safety. On balance, it came out to a plus. Barely.

Erin parked in the police space near the pub, got Rolf in hand, and went in. The place was full of big tattooed guys with a scattering of girlfriends. They were watching a martial-arts match on the bar's big-screen TVs, cheering a pair of sweaty, muscular goons who were beating the crap out of each other.

She threaded through the crowd to the bar. There sat Carlyle, slender, handsome, impeccably dressed in his customary suit and tie, elbows on the bar, watching the room. He saw her immediately, and Erin felt a rush of pleasure at the way his eyes lit up. He stood as she approached, always the old-school gentleman.

"Erin, darling," he said. "I'd hoped to see you, but I'd no idea you were coming around this afternoon. I'd thought you'd be visiting with your mum and da, seeing as they're in town. What can I get for you?"

She flashed him a smile. "Nothing for me, thanks. I'm working."

His smile didn't falter, but his eyes became concerned, almost wary. "As am I, darling. It's a shame the city doesn't permit you the same latitude it extends to publicans."

"You really think that's a good idea?" she replied. "A bunch of cops getting boozed up and running around Manhattan armed to the teeth?"

"It wouldn't be the first time it's happened in this fair city."

"That doesn't make it smart."

He nodded. "What's this about, then?"

"I think you already know." Carlyle's sources of information were quick and competent. Erin suspected she wasn't the only voice from the NYPD that came to his ears.

"The unpleasantness in Little Italy?"

"Yeah."

"I don't know that I can be much assistance on the subject."

"Marco Conti," she said.

He raised an eyebrow. "What is it you're wanting to know?"

"Who is he?"

"I've no doubt your department has a file on him."

"So he's a wiseguy."

Carlyle smiled thinly. "Did I say that?"

Erin smiled back. She wouldn't admit it, but she'd gotten to enjoy their verbal fencing matches. "You said we had a file on him."

"Your department has files on a number of citizens," he observed. "Not all of them are in the Life."

"But Conti was."

"I see you're speaking of him in the past tense."

"Does that bother you?"

Carlyle's shoulders moved in the slightest hint of a shrug. "Not particularly."

"He was a Lucarelli," she said, marveling at the way they could have a conversation like this in the middle of a crowded bar. The noise and activity around them acted as a screen, giving them a weird privacy in plain view.

He nodded. "I'd say that's common knowledge."

"He got whacked today," she went on. "Thoroughly."

"In my experience," he said dryly, "that sort of thing is either successful, or it's not."

"Someone wanted him dead bad enough to take down a whole building, and everyone inside it."

"How are you sure he was the intended recipient, if that's the case?"

"They were waiting for him. They torched the joint, and when he ran out the back, a triggerman was waiting. He was targeted. Specifically."

"What is it you're wanting from me, Erin?"

"I want to know what Conti was into," she said. "What side of the Lucarelli business did he work? Who wanted him out of the picture? Was it an internal job, or someone from outside his family? And what the hell did he do that warranted burning a whole building and killing a bunch of people just to get to him? They had to know the kind of heat that'd bring down. This is going to be a top priority. I mean, straight up to the Commissioner."

Carlyle rubbed his chin. "I see your point," he said quietly. "I'd no dealings with the man. His business is—was, I should say—the import and distribution of the sort of item you encountered the last time you brushed up against his people."

Erin nodded. Her previous encounter with the Lucarellis had been a drug bust. Acting on a tip from one of Carlyle's contacts in the O'Malleys, she'd worked with the Street Narcotics Enforcement Unit to seize a clean million dollars' worth of heroin.

"How much pull did he have?" she asked.

"It's my understanding that if you wanted to invest in a good horse in Little Italy, he was a fine lad to know," he said, using one of the many street euphemisms for heroin.

"Have you heard anything about a drug war? Anything getting talked about on the street?"

He shook his head. "As you know, Erin, I keep well clear of the stuff."

"But your people don't," she said. "What about Liam?"

Liam McIntyre was the O'Malley narcotics man. Erin had met him twice. He hadn't made a good impression either time, but he'd been useful in tipping her off to the drug shipment she'd taken down.

"Are you asking me what he knows, or are you asking me to set up a meeting with him?"

"Either. Both."

"I'll see what I can do," Carlyle said. "It may take a day or two, but I imagine I can sit the two of you down somewhere."

"Do that," she said. "I've got a feeling this might have something to do with what happened in February."

"Continuation of the unpleasantness surrounding the loss of their product, you mean?"

"Maybe," she said. "We're not ruling anything out. Mostly I need to know if this was a one-off, or if there's going to be more bodies getting dropped."

"I understand your concerns. I'm afraid I've no idea what goes through Liam's head these days, though I've a suspicion more than a little of his own product goes up his nostrils. The lad would hardly confide in me. He's more comfortable with the likes of Mickey and Miss Blackburn."

Erin suppressed a shudder. She'd met both the O'Malley associates he'd named. Mickey Connor in particular was a nasty piece of work. "I don't want to see Mickey," she said. "Just Liam. Set it up."

"I'll be about it," he said. "Does that conclude our business?"

"I think that's it for now."

"Then I'm thinking it's time for that drink I offered you when you came in."

Erin smiled. "Sorry. Still on duty."

"Erin, it's past eight. How long have you been working?"

"It's my day off, so I didn't exactly clock in. But I'm not done yet. At least I'm used to working nights."

"I live by night, too, as you're well aware. Perhaps I'll see you later on? I can come by your flat, if you're wanting a bit more peace and quiet than you'd find hereabouts."

"That'd be nice."

"When should I drop by?"

"I'll call you." She didn't bother to ask if he'd still be up. He usually went to bed well after midnight.

"That reminds me," he said. "I've a new number."

Erin fished out her phone and pulled up his contact info. He was listed on her device as "CI" for "Confidential Informant," with no other identifying information. Cautious man that he was, he insisted on changing burner phones every couple of weeks. On top of that, she knew he kept a couple of clean phones nearby for extra-sensitive business.

"Some people might think you were a little paranoid," she said, replacing the old phone number and saving the update.

"Aye, they might," he said. "But I'd remind them I'm an old gangster. That's a mark of distinction. There are a great many young gangsters. The mathematics speak for themselves. You want to talk about paranoia? I'm living on top of a public house. The Corner was a speakeasy back in the Prohibition days, did you know?"

"I didn't," she said with a smile. "But it doesn't surprise me. You're carrying on the old bootlegger tradition?"

"Aye. They operated out of the cellar. Secret passages and the like, all manner of subterfuge. There's even a hidden entrance to the building."

"How mysterious," she said with a grin. It actually was kind of romantic, now that she thought about it. "I'll give you a ring."

"I'll be waiting."

*   *   *

Carlyle was right. It was late, and Erin had no wish to go back to the office, but this wasn't an ordinary evening. A gangland shootout that left multiple bodies and a burnt-out building was going to get a lot of attention. Until they cleared the case, they'd all be working whenever they could.

Erin tried to muster up her usual enthusiasm for the chase. Rolf was on board with the plan, eager and energetic, but what she really wanted was to go home and relax on the couch. A glass of Carlyle's top-shelf whiskey in her hand, Carlyle giving her shoulders a massage with his gentle, clever fingers, and some soft music on the stereo sounded a lot better than doing detective grunt-work all night.

"But that's the job we've signed up for," she said to her partner. Rolf cocked his head and perked his ears, giving her a quizzical expression. Of course this was what he'd signed up for. No question.

So back to the precinct they went. Erin parked her Charger in the underground garage and took the elevator up to the second-floor Major Crimes office.

The doors opened on semi-organized chaos. She'd expected activity, but this was something else. Uniformed officers swarmed around the desks, with a sprinkling of plainclothes detectives, most of them strangers. She saw a cluster of guys wearing DEA jackets near the windows, a couple of FBI guys hanging around outside Captain Holliday's office, and some other Feds at Webb's desk talking to Vic and the Lieutenant. Among them, she saw a familiar face.

"Agent Johnson," she said, coming up behind him. "I didn't know Homeland was interested in this."

Paul Johnson, Homeland Security, turned toward her with a friendly smile. "Detective O'Reilly!" he said, offering his hand. "Glad you're with us. Your partner, too," he added, winking at Rolf.

Erin shook hands gladly enough. Agent Johnson, unlike too many other Feds, believed in genuine cooperation between agencies. He'd been helpful in stopping a terrorist plot the previous year. But she didn't understand why Homeland would be here now.

"We were tracking a person of interest," Johnson said. "I was just filling in your commanding officer. Most of the details are classified..."

"Naturally," Vic interjected.

"...but I can tell you he's associated with an organization of particular interest to my agency," Johnson finished, ignoring the interruption.

"Conti's a terrorist?" Erin said incredulously. "He was Mafia."

"Conti?" Johnson repeated. "Who's Conti? Oh, right, one of your victims. I'm not talking about him."

"You got an ID on someone else who was there?" Vic asked.

"Diego Rojas."

"That's not an Italian name," Webb observed.

"He's Colombian," Johnson said. "Or he was. I suspect he's no longer living. I need to confirm his death. Then I'll be out of your hair."

"But he was in the restaurant?" Webb asked.

Johnson nodded. "We had intel he would be meeting with someone there today."

"What about?" Webb asked.

"We don't know. Probably some sort of narcotics deal."

"Since when does Homeland Security give a shit about the War on Drugs?" Vic asked. "Aren't you too busy losing the War on Terror?"

"One war at a time," Johnson agreed good-naturedly. "And I could say you're not doing much better with the drugs. But the Black Falcons, the group Rojas represents, occupy a gray area. They're a paramilitary organization that finances itself with the drug trade. They're not terrorists, technically, but we're keeping an eye on them just in case."

"I hope we can get you your guy," Webb said.

"I hope not," Johnson said ruefully. "We've been hoping Rojas would lead us to other contacts, helping us develop a sense of the Falcons' reach in America. Instead, we've got a dead end. So to speak."

"We're not going to be pulling any live bodies out of the scene," Webb agreed. "FDNY is still trying to sort out the count."

"In the meantime, what can you tell us about Rojas?" Erin asked. "I know, I know, it's mostly classified. But there has to be something."

"We think he's a negotiator with the Falcons," Johnson said. "We know he brokered deals with drug dealers in Miami and Tampa last year. That's why he was so valuable to us. We wanted to let him run loose for a while, see who he led us to."

"That explains the DEA," Vic said, pointing a thumb at the agents at the window. "Give those guys a sniff of heroin, it gives 'em all hard-ons, especially interstate operations."

"We got NYPD Narcos here, too?" Erin asked Webb.

He nodded. "They're talking to the Captain in his office."

"You talk to Holliday?" she asked.

"Only for a minute," Webb said. "There's a line around the block to talk to him. This one's got all kinds of pressure. It's not as bad as the City Center thing last year, but you know how it goes."

"Shit rolls downhill," Vic said sourly.

"The Captain gave me two sentences," Webb said. "He said, and I quote, 'Get these guys. Anything you need, I'll get it for you.'"

"Unlimited overtime," Vic said. "That's the first good news today. I've been looking at a PS4 for my man cave."

"Vic," Erin said. "How big is your apartment?"

"It's a studio."

"How can you have a man cave in a one-room apartment?"

He shrugged. "It's pretty much all cave. With a bed in the corner."

"I'm surprised you don't sleep on the floor. You got a kitchen, or do you eat your meals raw?"

"I'll talk to my people," Johnson said, steering the conversation back to the case. "We'll have to redact the file a little, but I'll send you what I can. If you can let me know as soon as you ID the bodies?"

"Will do," Webb said. He shook hands with the agent, who turned to go, accompanied by a pair of silent, black-suited fellow agents.

"That takes care of Homeland Security," Vic said, once they'd left. "Don't you feel more secure, knowing they're here?"

"They don't care about this case," Erin said. "They just care about their guy."

"It's interesting, though," Webb said thoughtfully. He turned to Erin. "What were you able to find out from your CI?"

"Not a whole lot," she said. "I did hear Conti was a player in the heroin market."

"Sounds like he may have been making a deal with this Rojas character," Webb said.

"Maybe someone didn't want the deal to go through," she replied.

"Or it was an unrelated hit on Rojas. Or Conti. Or both." Vic frowned.

"I'm going to meet with another contact tomorrow, or maybe the day after," she said. "Maybe he can tell me more."

"Good," Webb said. "We don't want a drug war breaking out here. It'll be just like the Eighties with crack."

"I was in grade school in the Eighties," Erin reminded him.

"And I was in Los Angeles," he replied. "I was a new boot, a rookie fresh out of the Academy, working Patrol. We picked up a lot of bodies back in those days."

"I don't believe it," Vic said. "You were never a boot. You've always been a middle-aged gumshoe."

"Neshenko," Webb said, looking at him as if he'd just remembered he was there. "Don't you have some use-of-force paperwork to fill out?"

Vic muttered something unintelligible.

"Care to repeat that?"

"I said, doesn't the high profile of this case take priority over routine paperwork, sir?"

Erin was pretty sure that wasn't what Vic had said the first time.

"Good point," Webb said. "This is a high-profile investigation, which means there'll be more than the usual scrutiny. Which means someone will wonder exactly what Detective Neshenko was shooting at in that burning building."

"I'll get on the paperwork," Vic growled, slouching off to his desk like an oversized scolded schoolboy.

"The Captain's going to give a statement to the press in time for the ten o' clock news," Webb said to Erin. "It won't be anything substantial."

"Our investigation is ongoing?" Erin guessed. "No effort will be spared, et cetera?"

"Something like that. He's doing high-level liaison work with all these alphabet agencies. I need to coordinate manpower on the ground. You need any bodies? I can throw some Patrol cops your way."

"I need a Narcotics detective," she said. "Someone who knows Little Italy."

"I'll talk to SNEU," Webb said.

"I actually know a guy there," she said.

Webb raised his eyebrows. "Really? How?"

"We did some stuff together," Erin said. She didn't want to explain she'd done an extracurricular drug bust in February. Her reasons for evading the question were that she hadn't gotten Webb's permission, or even informed him, and a guy had been murdered over it immediately afterward. She hadn't gotten him killed, not directly, but it was weighing on her conscience.

"I have to say, for a cop who's been a gold shield less than a year, you've got a pretty good network set up," he said. "By all means, call your guy. I'll give you any top cover you need. I can probably get him detailed to you, at least for a while."

"That might be helpful," she said. "He's got a good team. But right now I just need to pick his brain."

"Pick away. Is this guy a street officer?"

"Yeah."

"That's fortunate. Sensible people are home and getting ready for bed. He may still be working. Drop him a line, we'll see if we can get him in here."

Chapter 4

"Detective O'Reilly. Get bored behind that desk of yours?"

"Sergeant Logan," Erin said, standing up and offering her hand.

The Street Narcotics Enforcement Unit man grinned and shook with her. He was dressed for work, which meant jeans, sneakers, and a T-shirt topped with a beat-up leather jacket. He looked around the room at the representatives of various city and Federal agencies.

"I get why these guys are here," he said. "Why me? I got a buy and bust going down in an hour. Piekarski's gonna kick my ass if I'm not there."

"You outrank Piekarski," she reminded him.

He shrugged. "In the office, sure. On the street, depends on the situation. We got a saying in SNEU: a beat cop on the move outranks a sergeant who doesn't know what's going on. And that's me right now. What's the score, Detective?"

"Thanks for coming in, Sergeant," Webb said. "And I know you're busy, so we do appreciate this."

"Sure thing," Logan said, looking Webb up and down. "And you'd be...?"

"My commanding officer," Erin said. "Lieutenant Webb, Sergeant Logan."

"Gotcha. Pleasure, Lieutenant." Logan immediately turned back to Erin. "So, you were saying?"

"We're working the Little Italy firebombing," Erin said. "We think it was connected to a possible drug deal. I wanted to see what you can tell me about the players in the area."

"Who's the victim?"

"A Lucarelli associate, name of Marco Conti."

"The Mouth?"

"I'm sorry?" Erin didn't quite follow.

"Marco the Mouth. Talkative guy, I guess."

"So you know him?"

"Yeah. He moves a lot of product for the Lucarellis." Logan hesitated. "Not anymore, sounds like."

"He caught one in the head outside the restaurant," Erin confirmed. "Along with two others, his bodyguards we think."

"He was the mark?"

"Looks like it. Who's his competition?"

Logan rubbed the back of his neck. "Geez, O'Reilly, you want the phone book? There's the other four families, for starters. Then you got the Colombians, the Mexican cartels, half a dozen major street gangs, the Irish... It was easier back when it was just the Mob, y'know?"

"You saying monopolies have advantages?" Erin teased.

"It's the natural end point of capitalism, without government interference."

"But we are the government."

"Exactly. Busting up the five families with RICO made things a lot more complicated."

"Okay," Erin sighed. "You know anyone who had a particular beef with Marco, or with the Lucarellis in general?"

"Depends," Logan said. "We talking business, or revenge?"

"Could be either."

"Well, if it's business, could be any of the guys I just said. If it's revenge... Can't think of anyone off the top of my head. The Mouth is... was a popular guy. He didn't have any personal enemies I know of."

"You think maybe someone might've been trying to send a statement to the Lucarellis?" Erin guessed. "This was a pretty definitive hit, lots of collateral damage."

"Hell of a statement," Logan agreed. "Tell you what. I'll keep my ear to the ground, see what the street's saying the next couple of days. You can bet the Italians are gonna be going crazy over this."

"Firelli's going to be buying a lot of drinks," Erin said.

Logan laughed at the reference to his Italian squad member. Logan's team had a tradition where its Italian member paid for drinks when they busted Italians. Logan, being Irish, had to buy when they took down his own countrymen.

"Sorry to keep you off the street," she said. "But if you do hear anything, let me know."

"Will do. And if you get any juicy narcotics action, remember who loves you." Logan winked. "Catch you streetside, O'Reilly."

"Be safe," she replied.

Webb watched him go. "Cowboys," he muttered.

"They get results," Erin said, feeling a little defensive on Logan's behalf.

"They get headlines," Webb retorted. "Buy and bust, small-time stuff. They take low-level dealers off the street, and new guys take over their corners before the arrests are even processed. They don't make a damn bit of difference."

"That's police work," Erin said. "You see us running out of criminals any time soon, sir?"

A thin but genuine smile crossed Webb's face. "I see you've still got your idealism, O'Reilly. That's good. Hold onto it."

"I get it from my partner," she said, scratching Rolf behind the ears. "He never gives up."

"That's because it's all a game to him," Vic said, catching the tail end of their conversation. "I'm the same way. I'm still a cop 'cause I'm still having fun."

"And you have no other marketable skills," Erin said.

"That's not true!" Vic said. "I can do lots of stuff."

"Such as?"

"I'm a great shot. I'm good in a fistfight. I'm an expert at ESU tactics, especially dynamic entry. I'm proficient in long and short firearms. I've got a brown belt in krav maga..." He paused and sighed. "Okay, you're right. I can't do anything else."

"There's always the private sector," Webb said.

"Maybe once I put in my twenty," Vic said. "By then maybe I'll be tired enough of government guys and go be a security consultant for wealthy hedge-fund managers. They'll still be assholes, but they'll be a different flavor."

Webb winced. "Flavored assholes, Neshenko?"

"When you eat shit for a living, you acquire the taste," Vic replied.

Webb's phone buzzed. He held up a hand for the other two to be quiet. "Webb here. Yeah? You sure? Okay, thanks."

He hung up and looked at them. "That was the search-and-rescue boys. They think they've got all the bodies out of the restaurant. They won't be able to ID them for a while, of course."

"What's the damage?" Vic asked.

"In addition to the three out back, we got seven more from inside."

Vic whistled softly. "Seven?"

"Some of them are going to be civilians," Erin said.

"I know." Webb didn't look happy. "That's ten fatalities. *Ten.* That's a damn massacre."

*   *   *

After talking with Logan, there wasn't much left for Erin to do. Detectives spent a depressing amount of time waiting for people to get back to them. Vic went out to Little Italy to pound pavement and ask around, in the hopes that someone might have seen something. Levine was in the morgue, working her way through the ugly task of identifying seven badly burned corpses. Erin wandered down to see how the medical examination was getting on, telling Rolf to stay by her desk. The Shepherd obediently settled on his makeshift bed for a nap.

The smell stopped her in the morgue's doorway. The room usually smelled of disinfectant and formaldehyde, with underlying decay. Erin wasn't accustomed to the scent of an overcooked barbecue. There was actually smoke in the air, and knowing it was particles of the victims themselves didn't make her feel any better. She knew that smell was going to linger in her hair for days. She was glad she'd left Rolf upstairs. She hadn't forgotten about the bath he still needed.

"Hey, Doc," she called.

"What?" Levine was bent over one of the victims, taking a picture of the body's face. She didn't look up.

"How're you coming on the IDs?" Erin took a cautious step into the room, one hand clamped protectively over her nose and mouth.

"We'll need to use dental records," Levine said. "Fingerprints are unusable, due to the incineration of soft tissue."

"Did they have wallets, anything in their pockets?"

"Some of them," Levine said. "But the heat was sufficient to melt plastic, so driver's licenses and credit cards didn't survive. I'm sending dental X-rays to dentists in the greater New York area for potential matches."

Erin sighed. "We think some of these guys might be internationals."

"I may be able to ascertain that from dental evidence," Levine said.

"Yeah, I remember you did that with that Russian girl last year," Erin said. "Could you tell if dental work got done in, say, Colombia?"

"Colombia is known for dental tourism," Levine said.

"That's not what I do on vacation," Erin said.

"It's much cheaper abroad," Levine explained. "Especially without insurance. Unfortunately, the procedures themselves are very similar to those done in the United States. I doubt that will be helpful for establishing country of origin."

"If we get a miss on the dental records, what will you do?" Erin asked with a sinking feeling.

"DNA," Levine said, confirming Erin's fears.

"What's the current backlog?"

"Four months."

"We don't have four months. We have to know who these people are now."

Levine shrugged. "I can't rush the process. Maybe your commander can get it moved forward in line, but it'll still be a month or two. What do you know about them?"

"Some of them probably worked at the restaurant. We'll have locations where the bodies were found. Can you at least tell me whether they're male or female?"

"Certainly. Six men, one woman."

"Okay, that's a start. Find out everything you can about these people, and keep us posted."

"I can get you blood types within twenty-four hours, and tissue samples now. If you can get me other samples for comparison, I can do a DNA match between them in seventy-two hours."

"Levine, if we had samples, we'd already know who they were."

Levine shrugged again. "I can't change the science."

Erin went back upstairs, glad to get out of the smoky room. But the smell clung to her and followed her up the elevator.

*   *   *

Erin thought about what Levine had said. Maybe they could get something from the crime scene. She called up the New York Department of Transportation and, after the requisite automated menu and wait on hold, ended up talking to one of the traffic camera supervisors.

"Yeah, Detective, we're workin' that thing your people sent us," he said. "We got a car for your gunmen. It's a Dodge Caravan, black. No positive IDs on the guys. Looks like they tinted the windows past the legal limit. We sent the plates over a few minutes ago."

"Good, thanks," Erin said. "But I'm actually calling about something else. Can you send the traffic cam footage from before the incident? Say, everything from the preceding half hour, the cameras on both sides of the restaurant?"

"Sure, no problem. You know what vehicle you're trying to ID?"

"No."

"Okay, I'll get you the footage. Give me ten or fifteen minutes, I'll send it."

Erin hung up and walked over to Webb's desk. "You got the plates on the getaway car?" she asked.

He nodded but didn't seem excited. "Yeah. They're registered to a Subaru Outback belonging to a Daisy Langley. She lives in Brooklyn. I just called her, and it turns out she's out of the country, building houses for Habitat for Humanity in Haiti."

"Stolen plates?" Erin asked.

"Stolen plates," he agreed. "Her car's parked at JFK, according to her husband. Without its plates, I expect."

"So, that's a dead end," she said.

Webb nodded again. "Worth a try. It just confirms this was a professional hit."

Once she had the traffic video files on her computer, Erin settled down for some boring movie-watching. She wasn't sure exactly what she was looking for, but trusted her Patrol instincts to nudge her if anything was out of place.

Sure enough, a few minutes before the shooting started, a black SUV drove through the intersection south of the crime scene. The driver and passenger both had black, slicked-back hair and sunglasses. That wasn't strange. What was strange was when she saw the same vehicle go through the next intersection two minutes later, without the passenger, circling the block. Probably looking for a parking spot, or maybe loitering in the vicinity of the meeting.

Erin saved screenshots of the car and sat back from her computer. She'd been hoping to identify a parked car at the scene, and maybe be able to get vehicle registration and DNA samples from it, but this could be just as good. Now she had faces, a potential victim and a potential associate, and a car and license plate to go with them. She ran the plate and got a rental agency at JFK airport. She called them immediately. It was after midnight, but airport rentals were open twenty-four seven.

After another obligatory automated menu and few minutes on hold, the line was picked up by a guy. His voice was flat and hopeless. She'd heard livelier sounds coming out of the morgue.

"Speedy Rentals, Carl speaking. Do you have a reservation?"

"Hi, Carl," Erin said brightly, trying to inject some energy into him. "My name's Detective O'Reilly. I'm with NYPD Major Crimes. I need to ask you some questions about a rental."

"What's your reservation number, ma'am?" he droned on.

Erin stopped, took a breath, and tried again. "Carl!" she barked. "I'm Erin O'Reilly. I'm a cop. Major Crimes. I need you to wake up now."

"Huh? Oh... yeah. Sorry. Look, uh... sir? Ma'am? What do I call you?"

"Detective will do fine."

"Okay, yeah. Detective. Uh... I should get Mr. Talbot."

"Who's Mr. Talbot?"

"My manager."

"Yeah, Carl, I think maybe you should."

"Uh... here's the thing. He's... uh... not here."

"Where is he?"

"Uh... he went on, like, a coffee break."

"When do you think he'll be back, Carl?"

"I dunno."

Erin prayed to Saint Michael, patron of police, for patience. "When did he go on break?"

"Uh... about nine o' clock."

"Carl," she said. "That was three hours ago. That's a pretty long coffee break. I don't think Mr. Talbot is coming back."

"You think so?"

"I think it's just you and me, Carl."

She heard his nervous gulp even over the phone. "Okay," he said. He now sounded completely awake, and like he'd rather be somewhere else. "Look, lady... Detective, I mean... I don't wanna get in trouble here. I need this job."

"No trouble, Carl," she said, making her voice as soothing as she could. "I've got a license plate for a black Toyota 4Runner, plate number BPC 2987. I just need to know who rented it."

"That's personal information, Detective," Carl said, and despite herself, Erin was a little impressed at the way he managed to put some backbone into his answer. "Look, I... like I said, I don't wanna get in trouble, but I don't know if you're really a cop, okay? And even if you are, I can't give you that without a court order."

"Okay, Carl. How long is your shift?"

"I'm here until four." He said it like a convict less than halfway into a long prison sentence.

"Okay, I'm going to e-mail you the document in a few minutes. Then I'm going to call you back."

"Okay," Carl said, sounding a little more cheerful.

"Carl," Erin said, her police instincts tingling, "you're going to answer the phone when I call back, right?"

"Uh... yeah. Of course."

"You're not going to go on a coffee break yourself, are you?"

"No." But the spark had gone back out of his voice.

"Because we'll come and get you if you go. You know how many cops there are in New York City? Think carefully."

"I'll be here."

"That's good, Carl." Erin hung up and called Judge Ferris.

Police, as a general rule, distrusted judges. Erin's dad liked to call them lawyers who played dress-up, and no good cop was keen on lawyers. But Ferris was a useful contact for law enforcement. No one knew just how old he was; seventy-five was Erin's guess. He slept most of the afternoon, but tended to be up late. He was a judge who believed in law, order, and a good police force. He could be counted on to sign off on most warrants and court orders, as long as he was awake.

She was in luck. Ferris answered on the fourth ring. His voice was mellow, with the gravelly undertone of an old man who'd smoked a lot in his youth. It reminded her of the actor James Coburn.

"Good evening," he said.

"Evening, Judge," she said. "This is Detective O'Reilly."

"Ah, the charming Miss O'Reilly. And how are you this fine evening, young lady?"

"I'm good. Say, I'm not disturbing you, am I?"

"I'm just sitting here in my parlor with a few close and intimate friends, in front of a warm fire."

"Oh, I'm sorry. Should I call back later?"

"No, young lady, my friends are patient and reliable. Their names are Elijah Craig, Nat Sherman Sterling, Samuel Clemens, and Roy Bean."

Erin tried to make sense of what he'd just said. Elijah Craig was a whiskey brand, and Samuel Clemens sounded familiar. The other two were strangers. Then she placed Clemens. "You're reading Mark Twain and drinking bourbon," she guessed.

"With a fine cigar and my loyal dog at my feet," Ferris confirmed. "All that was missing for my contentment was the conversation of a fine young woman. Thanks to you, my evening is now complete. How may I be of service?"

She smiled. "I need a court order, Judge."

"Would this pertain to that terrible business this afternoon?"

"It would. I got a rental car on traffic cams, driving past the crime scene and dropping off at least one passenger right before the shooting. I need an order to get the rental record."

Ferris paused, and Erin could picture him taking a sip of his excellent top-shelf bourbon. "You think this information will be useful? Surely, if this vehicle was rented by an assassin, he would have taken pains to disguise his identity."

"I think it's one of the victims, not the killer."

"Ah. That casts the issue in a different light. I shall be delighted to assist you."

"I'll send the info to you. Thanks."

"I am, as ever, as your service. Have a very pleasant night, Miss O'Reilly."

A few minutes later, armed with Ferris's signed order, Erin called Speedy Rentals back. The unfortunate Carl answered.

"Speedy Rentals, Carl speaking. Do you have a reservation?"

"Hi, Carl. This is Detective O'Reilly. Did you get my e-mail?"

"Yes."

"Well?"

"That 4Runner was rented yesterday... by a Diego Rojas."

Bingo, Erin thought. "Thanks, Carl," she said. "Did he pay cash?"

"Yes."

"Okay, thanks." Erin hung up and looked at the clock on the wall. It said 12:55. Rolf, his chin between his paws, looked expectantly up at her.

"I know," she said to him. "I don't want to be here either."

What she wanted was to call Carlyle, have a drink, and relax. What she did instead was call Agent Johnson.

"Johnson." He sounded wide awake and alert. Erin wondered if Homeland Security guys ever slept, or if they just plugged batteries into the backs of their skulls.

"Erin O'Reilly," she said. "I got a hit on Diego Rojas."

"Talk to me."

"He rented a car at JFK, Toyota 4Runner, black, BPC 2987. Paid in cash, yesterday."

"O'Reilly?"

"Yeah?"

"We know about that already."

"Oh." Erin felt suddenly stupid. Of course Homeland Security would know. They were following Rojas and he'd used his own name to rent the car. What a waste of an evening.

"Good follow-up, though," Johnson said. "How'd you tumble to that?"

"I got some traffic cam footage with that car outside the restaurant."

"Yeah, we figured. Like I told you, we thought he was meeting with the Italians. At least you've confirmed he was probably there. You know if he's one of the dead guys?"

"Not sure," she said. "I don't suppose you guys have a DNA sample we could run on the bodies?"

"We're working on that," Johnson said. "If I can swing it, I'll make sure it gets to your medical examiner."

"Agent Johnson?"

"Yeah?"

"There anything else I should know about Rojas?" She didn't add, "So we don't chase our tails any more than we have to," but was pretty sure he heard it in her voice.

"He flew into JFK out of Bogota yesterday with three associates: Sebastian Alvarez, Javier Montero, and Francisco Contreras. All of them are known narcotics guys, cartel connected. Alvarez and Contreras are sicarios, hitmen."

"You let guys like that just fly into my city?" Erin demanded. "And you call yourselves Homeland Security!"

Johnson didn't take the bait. "I told you, we were letting Rojas run in the hope he'd lead us to bigger game. I'm sorry it worked out this way. Do you think Rojas and his team were the shooters, or the targets?"

"I'm thinking targets," she said. "But we're still trying to sort out what happened."

"Tell you what," Johnson said. "I don't need to do this, and it's a little outside our usual line, but I'll send you pictures of these bad guys. Maybe your doc can match them to the bodies. Believe me, if Rojas is dead, we want to know it. We also want to know who killed him."

"Okay, thanks," Erin said. "For a government goon, you're not half bad."

"And you're okay, for a flatfoot gumshoe," Johnson volleyed back. "Good working with you, O'Reilly. Check your e-mail."

Sure enough, a message popped up in her inbox with several pictures attached. She opened them up on her monitor, flicking back and forth between the new images and the traffic camera footage.

"Thanks," she said again. "Yeah, two of these guys are the ones in the front seat of the rental car. Rojas is driving, Contreras is riding shotgun."

"Great," Johnson said. "Let me know once you've got confirmed ID on your stiffs. See you on the flip side."

Erin fired off the pictures to Levine. Then, finally, she shut down her computer and pushed back from her desk. Rolf immediately sprang to his feet, tail wagging. He'd had a good nap and was ready for action.

"Lieutenant?" she called.

Webb held up a hand. He was on the phone with some agency or other. After a moment, he put the phone down and looked at her.

"I'm gonna bounce," she said. "I got possible IDs on four of our victims. I'll put them up on the board on the way out."

"See you tomorrow," Webb said. "Bright and early."

Then she and Rolf were free and clear, leaving the Major Crimes office behind. Erin had her phone up before she'd even gotten downstairs, calling Carlyle.

"Evening, darling," he said.

"Where are you?" she asked. She couldn't hear any of the usual background noise that would've indicated he was sitting in his usual spot at the bar.

"I'm up in my office, taking care of a few small matters. Is your business concluded for the night?"

"Yeah. Is yours?"

"Nothing that can't wait for tomorrow."

"I hate to break it to you, but it *is* tomorrow."

He laughed. "Fair enough. Shall we say, it can wait until I've slept on it."

"Planning on going to sleep?"

"Unless you've a better plan."

Erin smiled as she walked to her car. "I might."

"May I call on you in a short while?"

"Sure thing. I just have to get home, run Rolf around the block, and get cleaned up. I smell like a cookout."

"I'll be there in, shall we say, forty minutes?"

"Better make it an hour. I have to wash my dog."

* * *

"I still smell like charcoal," Erin said.

Carlyle kissed her neck just below her ear. "It's not as bad as you're thinking," he murmured. "The dirt we've got on ourselves is always more obvious to us than to everyone else."

"That's what you tell yourself?" she replied, curling herself against him. They were sitting on her couch, glasses of Glen D scotch on the table. Rolf, damp and bedraggled, sulked in the kitchen. The NYPD hadn't figured out how to train a dog to like being bathed.

"Aye," he agreed pleasantly. "My priest, on the other hand, tells me to stop sinning so much. Then he gives me a few Hail Marys and Our Fathers as penance."

"You do that?" she asked, straightening and turning to look at him.

"Aye," he said again. "Don't you? You're a Catholic lass."

"Well, yeah, but not regularly." In point of fact, Erin couldn't quite remember how long it'd been since she'd been to Confession. "You're one of *those* gangsters, huh?"

He raised an eyebrow. "Just what are you meaning by that, darling?"

"Commit crimes six days of the week, go to church, repent, and call it a wash?"

She'd said it in a half-joking tone, but Carlyle didn't smile. "You think a lad doesn't worry about his soul, just on account of being in the Life?" he asked quietly.

"No, that's not what I meant," she said. Then she paused. "Well, maybe it is. I don't know. I guess I don't quite see how you can go to church, doing... what you do."

"You told me I was a good man, once upon a time," he said.

"Yeah," she said. "But..."

He waited.

Erin laughed ruefully. "Okay, you're right. I'm prejudiced. And maybe I'm feeling a little weird, because I haven't gone to church in a while."

"You could come to Mass with me."

"This is a funny line of conversation from a guy who's hoping to get his girl in bed with him," she said.

Then he did laugh. "That's something I'm not meaning to say at Confession."

"Aren't you supposed to confess all your sins?"

"Aye, but I'll not lie to my priest, nor to God. I can only confess them if I'm repentant. I don't regret a moment of time I've spent with you, Erin."

She kissed him. "I bet you could talk your way out of Purgatory if you had to."

"Maybe," he said, his tone thoughtful. "I've talked my way out of rooms where I knew at least one lad meant to kill me. And those lads were a sight less forgiving than the Almighty. It's a fine skill, and one you'd do well to cultivate. You don't know when your life may depend on your ability to talk a gangster around to your point of view."

"I don't know how you do it," she said, resting her head on his shoulder. "Hang out with guys like that."

"You'd be surprised what you can do, when you've no other choice. And on that subject, I've spoken with Liam."

Erin sat up again. "You set up a meeting?"

"Aye. Not at the Corner, I fear. Mr. McIntyre is otherwise occupied tomorrow, but he's agreed to clear up a bit of time. He'll be at the Amsterdam Billiards Club over on Eleventh Street, expecting you at eleven."

"You think he's got anything useful for me?"

"We'll not know until we talk to him."

"You're planning on being there?"

"If you'll have me. Liam's a mite twitchy, as you well know, and he's not accustomed to talking to coppers under social circumstances. I'm thinking I can steady him down a bit."

"Should I meet you there?"

"I'm thinking that's best."

"How romantic," she said. "Inviting your girl to go hang out with a drug dealer the next morning."

"It's hardly my idea of fun either," he said. "But it's business. However, I did say business could wait for morning." He drew her in close.

Erin set aside her thoughts on the case and surrendered to the moment. Here and now, she was with the man she loved. That was good enough for her. Carlyle was right. Tomorrow could take care of itself.

Chapter 5

Erin woke to the harsh buzz of her alarm. She reflexively rolled over and stabbed a finger onto the snooze button. Beside her, Carlyle stirred slightly but didn't wake up. He was an alert, perceptive man, but he wasn't a morning person. She eased her way out from under the sheets and slipped into her running clothes. As she pulled on her sweats, she glanced back at the man sleeping in her bed.

It was crazy, she knew it. He shouldn't be there. She shouldn't have let him into her life, let alone her bedroom. But she couldn't help smiling at him. His face, so alert and watchful when he was awake, was relaxed. He looked younger when he was sleeping, more at peace with himself. And the fact that he trusted her enough to fall asleep in her apartment touched her. He lived in a damned reinforced fortress with armed men protecting him, but he let his guard down for her.

Erin shook her head. "Come on, boy," she whispered to Rolf, jingling his leash. He was already on his paws, ready and willing, the indignity of his bath forgiven.

She and her partner left her apartment building and started jogging, angling through the park across the street. A slim young man in a dark gray coat was standing by a park bench. He nodded politely as she passed him.

Erin skidded to a halt as recognition hit her. "Ian?"

"Ma'am."

She instinctively checked his hands. They were in his pockets, which could be because it was a brisk March morning, or he could be holding a pistol. Ian Thompson was one of Carlyle's guys, a bodyguard and driver. He was also a former Marine Scout Sniper and, according to Carlyle, the single most dangerous man in New York City.

He certainly didn't look dangerous. He was smaller than average, face neutral, manners flawless. He carried a sort of stillness with him. But Erin had been a cop for twelve years, and something about Ian set off all her street warning signals. He was a little *too* still, and under that stillness was tension, like a high-voltage cable.

It couldn't possibly be a coincidence that he was here, while his boss was sleeping inside. But he'd also protected Erin in the past, and had never been anything but polite. She honestly didn't know what to make of him, but couldn't help liking him a little.

"Just in the neighborhood?" she asked.

"Working, ma'am."

She gave him a look. "You haven't been out here all night, have you?"

Ian shrugged.

"It's thirty degrees," she said.

"After a while you don't notice the cold. It helps keep you awake, if you keep moving. I've been out on worse nights."

"You could get picked up for loitering."

"I move around."

"That's a little creepy."

"No excuse, ma'am. Sorry for disturbing you." He turned and walked away from her, along the sidewalk in front of her building.

Erin shook her head again. Carlyle trusted Ian completely, a rare thing in the Mob. If he wanted to spend all night on a Manhattan street, who was she to argue? And oddly, she did feel a little safer knowing he was out there. Rolf was looking at her, wagging his tail, ready for their run to continue. She obliged him.

* * *

She let herself back into the apartment, gave Rolf his breakfast, and climbed into the shower. By the time she came out, wrapping one towel around herself and another around her hair, Carlyle was up and pulling on his trousers. He'd been woken by the running water.

"Morning, darling," he said, coming over to give her a kiss. She ran her hands over his shoulders, savoring the feel of his skin against hers.

"Morning," she replied. "I ran into your boy Ian outside."

Carlyle sighed. "I told the lad he could go home. He seems to think I'm in some sort of danger."

"Aren't you always?"

"It's a matter of degrees. He's of the opinion the unsettled atmosphere in this city is making it more likely someone's intending to take a shot at me."

"Why you?" Erin asked. "You're not in the drug business."

"I asked him that myself," Carlyle said, buttoning his shirt. "He said incoming fire doesn't discriminate."

"Could just be hyperawareness," she said. "That happens to a lot of combat veterans. They get really nervous all the time, assuming threats are out there."

He nodded. "That doesn't make him wrong, but I imagine you're right. I'm not particularly worried. If I thought I'd bring trouble, I'd not have come to your home last night." He looped his necktie around his throat and knotted it with swift, skillful movements. "No matter how much I wanted to," he added.

"You want any breakfast?" she asked.

"I'll eat at the Corner." He tied his shoes, pulled on his coat, and walked to the door.

"See you in a couple of hours," she said. She caught him in the doorway and gave him one more kiss. He drew her into his arms and smiled. For just a moment, they were like any couple in love, heading off for work.

"Grand," he said. Then he was gone.

*   *   *

Levine had been up all night, working on the bodies the FDNY had pulled out of the wreckage. The fruits of her labor were waiting for Erin on her computer. While Erin was looking over the results, Webb stalked into the office.

"We've got IDs," Erin announced.

"Great," Webb said. "Coffee first." He disappeared into the break room. A minute later he was back with a steaming cup in his hand. "Sorry. City of New York won't let me smoke indoors, I have to get my stimulants somehow."

"They should put cocaine in the vending machine downstairs," Erin deadpanned.

"Bad idea. It already won't take money half the time. You'd have junkies breaking the glass every day. What've we got?" He walked to her desk and stood looking over her shoulder.

"Three of the burn victims are Colombian nationals," she said. "Sebastian Alvarez, Javier Montero, and Francisco

Contreras. They're known associates of Diego Rojas, the guy Agent Johnson was asking about."

"What about Rojas himself?" Webb asked.

"Looks like it was his lucky day. He's not one of our bodies. I guess he wasn't inside."

"Or he's still buried somewhere onsite," Webb suggested.

"The Colombians were found around this table," Erin went on, pointing to a floor plan of the building annotated by Levine. "There was a fourth body also at the table, but according to the doc, he's definitely not Rojas. She doesn't have a positive ID on him yet. All four also suffered multiple GSW, both ante- and post-mortem."

"The shooters kept firing after they were dead," Webb said. "Just to make sure."

"Well, one of them was shot twice several minutes after his heart stopped beating," she said.

"Ah." Webb put down his coffee and rubbed his temples. "That'd be Neshenko's one-sided gunfight."

"Yeah. At least he hit the guy he was aiming for. Of the other three bodies, two were in the kitchen, tentatively identified as cooks. Federico Greco and Cristian Rossi. No extra holes in them. Looks like cause of death was third-degree burns and smoke inhalation. Levine appended a report from Skip Taylor. Skip says the firebomb sent flames through the swinging doors and ignited a whole lot of shit in the kitchen, cooking oil and stuff. Apparently the gas stove blew up, too."

"Ouch," Webb said. "That'd do it."

"The last victim was the only woman," Erin finished. "Arianna Rossi. She died in the dining room, in the middle of the floor, shot to death."

"Same last name as one of the cooks," Webb observed.

"Probably related," Erin said, already checking the city records. "Yeah, looks like she's Cristian's daughter. It was a family restaurant. Geez, she was just seventeen."

Webb looked away and didn't say anything. Erin remembered he had a pair of daughters from his first marriage, probably about the same age as the victim.

"Okay," he said. "How firm are these IDs?"

"Levine's got our good facial-recognition program," she said. "She gave the Colombians a probable match of ninety-seven percent based on the photos I gave her. The others didn't actually get ID'd in the morgue. Vic talked to some folks in the neighborhood and figured out who was working that day. He shot Levine the names at three-thirty this morning. Levine says she's waiting on a DNA match or confirmation from relatives to be sure."

"I guess that's why Neshenko's not in yet," Webb said. "I'm surprised he bothered to go home at all."

Erin nodded and stood up. "That coffee smells too good," she said. "I'm getting some."

She walked through the break room's doorway, put a cup under the nozzle, and started filling it. Then she did a double take. She turned, looked at the couch for a moment, then went back to her drink. She came out and returned to her desk.

"Vic didn't go home," she informed Webb. "He's in the break room, on the couch."

"Oh."

"You didn't see him there?"

Webb shook his head.

"He's pretty big, sir."

"In my defense," Webb said, "I hadn't actually drunk any of my coffee yet." He thought it over. "Neshenko's on that couch?"

"Yeah. Should I wake him up?"

"I don't think I've ever been tired enough in my life to risk falling asleep on that thing," Webb said. "Let him rest."

*　　*　　*

There was a lot of activity in the Major Crimes office, but very little progress. Captain Holliday passed through on the way to his office, disappeared inside, and dove into an endless stream of telephone conversations. CSU techs kept showing up with new pieces of evidence from the scene, including some cartridge cases, bits of broken glass from the Molotov cocktails, and a blackened nine-millimeter automatic found on the floor near the dead Colombians. The detectives looked everything over as it arrived. The shell casings would be useful if they could match them to a weapon, but Erin was sure the perps had gotten rid of the guns.

Vic wandered out of the break room, rubbing his eyes, a little after nine. He stopped, stared at the window, and blinked.

"It's morning," he said, sounding surprised and a little offended.

"You noticed," Erin said.

"Solve the case yet?"

"We don't even have a suspect. We've just about identified all the victims."

Vic looked at the whiteboard, which Erin and Webb had updated with their new information. He stared at it for a long time.

"This wasn't a hit," he said at last.

Webb and Erin looked at each other, then back at him.

"I think I misheard you," Webb said. "Explain."

"The point wasn't to kill one of these guys," Vic said.

"It sure looked like it out back," Erin said.

"I don't think so," Vic said. "They want to kill one guy, why have their expert shooter waiting out back? Hell, they don't even know if he's gonna run that way. Nah, they wanna pop one guy, they send their ace right through the front door, smoke their target right in the face, use the firebombs to cover the retreat if they wanna torch the joint. The point wasn't to kill Conti. The point was to kill *everyone*."

"Why?" Webb asked.

"The hell do I know?" Vic replied. "Do I look like a hitman?"

"Kind of," Erin said.

"Not my point," Vic said.

"You kill one guy, it stops the drug deal," Erin said. "Temporarily. Wipe out the whole meeting, on both sides, it's likely to wreck the whole transaction."

"That makes as much sense as anything," Webb said. "Which means this could be the first shot in an out-and-out gang war."

"Or maybe not the first shot," Erin suggested.

"Good thought, O'Reilly," Webb said. "Take a look at recent gangland hits, especially anything Mafia-related. Maybe this is a retaliation, not a first strike."

So Erin scanned homicide case files until a little after 10:30, finding nothing unusual. Then she stood up.

"Going somewhere?" Vic asked.

"I've got a CI who might know what's going down in Little Italy. He said he'd meet me at eleven."

"Get us something," Webb said. "I hate organized crime hits. They're the hardest cases in the world to close."

"I don't think that's true, sir," she said. "Homicides in minority neighborhoods, especially in the poorer parts of Brooklyn—"

"If I wanted police stats, I'd have kept Jones in the department. I don't want to hear it, O'Reilly. I just want to solve this case."

*   *   *

Amsterdam Billiards was a corner lot with a wraparound light-up sign over the door. The joint was just opening when Erin and Rolf arrived. The billiard hall was dimly lit, finished in polished wood with a red carpet of interlocking circles. It was a little early in the day for playing pool, so the place was nearly deserted. Erin took her partner toward the bar, picking a spot where she could see the front door.

"Is that a service animal?" the girl behind the counter asked.

"Not exactly," Erin said. "Police K-9."

"Bad ass."

Rolf sat beside Erin and gave the girl a look as if to say that he was, indeed, a badass.

"Y'know, we don't have drugs or anything in here," the girl confided.

Erin raised her eyebrows.

"So there's nothing for him to sniff out," the girl explained.

"He's not a drug dog," Erin said.

"So, does he bite people?"

"Only the ones I tell him to."

"Bad ass," the girl said again.

The door swung open and Carlyle came in. He saw Erin and acknowledged her with a polite tilt of his head.

Behind him, Ian entered and stepped off to one side. The bodyguard swept the room with his eyes. Seeing nothing unusual, he took up a flanking position along the left-hand wall. He stood in an apparently relaxed posture, but Erin could see he wasn't quite leaning against the wall and was tenser than he looked.

"Morning, darling," Carlyle said, sliding into a seat next to her. "Have you ordered yet?"

"No, I just got here."

"Soda water with a dash of lime for me," he said to the bartender. "And I'll cover whatever she's having."

"Coke," Erin said. A little extra caffeine certainly couldn't hurt.

They got their drinks and sipped them. "Your kid over there had a late night," she observed, cocking an eyebrow Ian's way.

"Word on the street has it, the lad needn't sleep," Carlyle said.

"Like that thing he did in Afghanistan? I read his personnel file. But I don't believe it. He's got to sleep sometime." Erin was thinking of an incident during Ian's Marine days, in which he'd carried a wounded comrade for five days through hostile country. He'd been awake the whole time, so the story went.

"No fear, darling. He's sharp enough after one night's watching."

"So what about Liam? He going to show, or what?"

"Patience," Carlyle said. "He's not one by whom you can set a wristwatch. But he'll be here."

They waited.

"You think he knows anything useful?" Erin asked, eventually.

"I've no idea," Carlyle replied.

"How's Evan feel about us?"

He glanced at her. They hadn't talked much about her introduction to Evan O'Malley since she'd met Carlyle's boss about three weeks back.

"As I told you, he's favorably impressed," Carlyle said. "He thinks you're useful."

"Oh, good. I'm useful to a mob boss. Just what every cop wants."

"Need I remind you, Erin, this is precisely the outcome we wanted?"

She sighed. "You're right. It just takes a little getting used to. But he's okay with it? With you seeing me?"

"If not, he'd hardly tell me," Carlyle said. "He'd register his objections in an executive fashion."

Erin swallowed. She wasn't sure what to say to that.

She was saved from the conversation by Liam's arrival. The little, ferret-faced guy stepped through the door, glanced around, saw Erin and Carlyle, and scurried over to them. Halfway there, he paused and shot Ian a look. Ian returned it calmly. Then Liam got to the bar. He pulled himself onto a bar stool and tried to sit still.

It didn't work. His fingers drummed on the bar. His eyes, bloodshot and runny, flicked all over the room. Liam was never a relaxing guy to be around, but he struck Erin as particularly jittery today.

"Hey, man," she said. "Take it easy. Everything's cool."

"Yeah, yeah," he said. He sniffled and rubbed his nose. He looked at Erin with pupils that looked like big, black eightballs. She couldn't believe it. Eleven-fifteen in the morning and Liam was high as a kite.

"Thank you for meeting us, lad," Carlyle said. "We understand you're busy, and we appreciate it."

"Okay, sure," Liam said. "And I appreciate that thing last month."

"Forget about it," Erin said, giving the correct mob response. He was talking about the tip he'd given her which had led to the heroin shipment she and Sergeant Logan's team had taken down. "But anything else that's going on," she added, "we can talk."

"But in the meantime," Carlyle interjected, "there's something you may be able to help us with."

"What's that?" Liam asked. The bartender came over to see if they needed anything else. Liam started to wave her off, then changed his mind.

"You got milkshakes?" he asked.

"Sure."

"Okay, gimme three chocolate shakes and some of those brownies you got, the ones with the whipped cream."

The girl blinked. "I'm sorry, did you mean...?"

"I said three chocolate shakes, dammit!" he snapped. "Line 'em up on the bar, one, two, three. You think you can count that high, bitch?"

"Okay, okay!" she said. "Asshole," she added in an undertone as she moved off.

"Sorry," Liam muttered, turning back to Carlyle and Erin. "What was that?"

"Someone took down some Lucarellis pretty hard yesterday," Erin said. "I need to know who's got a beef with them."

Liam froze. For just a second, all his twitchy energy went totally still. Then he cocked his head and looked sidelong at Carlyle.

"The hell is this, Cars?"

Erin had gotten to know Carlyle pretty well, and she still had trouble seeing his surprise. Just a slight tightening of the skin around his eyes and his fingers curling a little more firmly around his glass of mineral water, that was all.

"I don't know what you mean, Liam."

"Why'd you bring her here? You said, like, she needed to talk to me. Okay, sure, I can talk, we can talk all day if you want, but y'know, we can only talk about this, not about that, y'know? I mean, how far in is she, really? Is she one of us, or one of them?"

"Lad," Carlyle said gently, "you're not making sense."

"You here as a cop?" Liam asked Erin.

"Yeah, I am."

Liam gave Carlyle a look that said "I told you so," even though he hadn't.

Erin shot Carlyle a confused look of her own. This was not going the way she'd expected. She tried to think what she could say.

"Look, Liam," she began. "If there's something going on I can help with, let me know. But you've got to talk to me, man. You don't want to name names, that's fine. But give me something I can use. We got a good relationship going here. I don't want to jeopardize that, and I know you don't, either."

But Liam stood up, quickly and abruptly. "Screw this, man," he said. "I gotta get outta here. Gotta get some air. Talk to you later, Cars."

He stumbled, almost fell, and scrambled out the door, nearly running.

Carlyle watched him go and turned to Erin. "I'm sorry, darling," he said. "I fear I've wasted all our time. I don't know what's come over the lad."

"What the hell?" the bartender demanded. She was standing there with the three milkshakes and the bowl of brownies Liam had requested. "He coming back?"

"I fear not," Carlyle said. "I apologize for him, ma'am. I'll cover his tab, naturally." He took out his wallet. Most mob guys carried their bills in a roll, but Carlyle was too classy for that. He fished out a couple of bills and slid them across the bar. "You needn't give me any change."

"Thanks," the bartender said, pocketing the bills. "Whatcha doing hanging out with a jerk like that, anyway?"

"More business than pleasure, I assure you," he said, turning his attention back to Erin. "I'm sure you'll be needing to get back to work. I don't suppose you're hungry?" He indicated the brownies.

"That guy's diet could give me diabetes just watching him eat," she said. But she picked up one of the brownies and moved it toward her mouth.

The sound from outside wasn't particularly loud, but it was distinctive. It was a rapid-fire series of rattling, popping sounds, a short burst followed by a longer one. A front window shattered, pebbles of tempered glass showering to the floor.

The bartender paused, staring in confusion. Erin and Ian were already moving, Carlyle a second behind them. Erin snatched out her Glock and ran toward the door. Rolf matched her stride for stride. Ian, with the smooth efficiency of a combat veteran, pulled a Beretta automatic from under his coat and, holding the gun in both hands, came to Carlyle's side.

"Move, sir," he said as Erin hurried past him. "Out the back. Now."

Erin didn't hear Carlyle's answer. What she heard was screams from outside the pool hall. "NYPD!" she shouted. She flung the door open and ran onto the sidewalk.

A ragged half-circle of New York pedestrians stood there, at a respectful distance from a crumpled shape. A pair of uniformed officers had just arrived. One of them knelt beside the body. The other stood with his sidearm in hand, waving the bystanders back with his other hand. As Erin approached, she heard the kneeling cop talking into his radio.

"We need a bus to 110 East 11th," he said. "Multiple GSW."

Erin flashed her shield to the standing officer. "O'Reilly," she said. "Major Crimes. What've we got?"

"Looks like a drive-by," he said. "Me and my partner was halfway down the block when we heard it. Shooter was already gone. Poor bastard probably never even knew what hit him."

Erin looked down. There, his blood outlining the channels in the concrete, lay Liam McIntyre. His eyes were wide open, staring at the sky, but he wasn't seeing anything in this world. A glance told Erin everything she needed to know. It didn't matter how fast the ambulance got there. He was already dead.

Chapter 6

Erin stood on Eleventh Street, her Glock in one hand, Rolf's leash in the other, trying to think. The adrenaline pumping through her veins didn't make it easier. Liam had been nervous during their abortive meeting. Had he known he was being targeted? That didn't make sense. Liam was the kind of guy who'd go to ground if he thought he was being hunted. He wouldn't stick his nose out of his hole.

Maybe it was a coincidence, an unrelated attack. Drug dealers ran a constant risk of being murdered by competitors. But Erin didn't believe in coincidence. Her father liked to say, *"Coincidence is like winning the lottery. How many people you know who've won the lottery?"*

At the moment, Erin had a more pressing concern. She needed to figure out what she was going to say to the Homicide detectives when they got there. If she even wanted to be there at all. Ian might've had the right idea. He and Carlyle were long gone by now.

Great, just great. She was thinking like a mobster. But she had to decide, and fast. For now, she was just an NYPD detective who'd happened to be in the vicinity of a gangland shooting. She didn't want her connection to the Irish Mob being talked about in another precinct. Next thing she knew, her relationship with Carlyle would come out, and then...

She didn't know what would happen then. Nothing good. But if the Homicide boys in Little Italy were any good at all, they'd trace Liam's movements prior to his death. They'd interview the bartender, who'd definitely remember the police officer and K-9. Then it would come back on Erin regardless.

So there wasn't really a choice. Besides, Sean O'Reilly hadn't raised his daughter to run and hide. And while she was biting bullets, she might as well get a whole mouthful. She called Webb.

"You talk to your guy?" he asked.

"Sort of."

There was a pause.

"You're going to have to explain that," he said. "Obviously."

"I met my CI," she explained. "But he got spooked and ran off."

"That actually sounds promising. Maybe this guy knows something. You think he'll crack if you lean on him a little?"

"That's the thing, sir. He didn't get far." She took a deep breath. "He's dead."

There was another pause. When Webb's voice came back on the line, he sounded enormously weary.

"Please tell me you didn't shoot him."

"What? No! But someone sure as hell did. Automatic fire, submachine-gun I think."

"Are you hit? Any other casualties?"

"No and no. I only heard it, I didn't see it happen. I'm at the scene with two uniforms, waiting on Homicide. I'll probably be tied up here for a while."

She heard the sigh over the phone line. "It is what it is," he replied. "Thanks for the heads-up. So now we have eleven bodies."

"That we know of."

"Thank you for that encouraging thought, O'Reilly. You think it's connected?"

"I don't see how it couldn't be."

"Same shooters as yesterday?"

"I only heard one gun. Couldn't say who did the shooting. They were gone by the time I got outside."

"Okay. Give my name to the Homicide boys when they show up, so we can coordinate who's going to work this one. It'll probably land on us, given the situation. But get back here as quick as you can. This one sounds like a misdemeanor."

Erin knew what he meant. Vic had used the same term to describe the Mafia guys. "Misdemeanor homicides" were what police called murders where the victims were criminals. They didn't tend to be the highest priority to solve, since they didn't directly endanger the public. If the firebombing hadn't killed civilians as well, the NYPD might not be bringing out its big guns to solve it.

"Copy that," she said. "O'Reilly out."

*   *   *

Erin didn't need to worry, as it turned out. The Homicide detectives, a couple of guys named Lawton and Crawford, only asked her a few perfunctory questions. She told them Liam was an informant, that he'd tipped her off to a competitor's drug deal a while ago, and she'd been meeting hoping to get some info on another case.

"He have anything for you?" Lawton asked.

"Nope," she said. "He got pissed off and left."

And that was it. Erin could see they'd already made up their minds about Liam. The story they were telling themselves was that he'd been on the bad side of some other drug dealer and gotten himself whacked. Open and shut. Not that they knew which dealer had killed him, but she figured they'd try to work that out later.

Erin left the scene feeling that Liam had gotten the sort of death he deserved. It didn't make her feel any better. She knew the shooting was linked to the restaurant massacre, but she didn't know how. All she knew for certain was that a potential lead had been cut off.

Her phone buzzed in her pocket as she was loading Rolf into her car. She saw an unknown number.

"O'Reilly," she said noncommittally.

"Are you well, darling?"

"Oh, it's you. New phone again?"

"Aye. Ian insisted. Once the lad gets going on the subject of operational security, it's difficult to convince him otherwise. I'd a spare in the car." Carlyle sighed. "I'd no wish to run out on you like that."

"I know. You did the right thing. You'd have gotten wrapped up in the investigation if you'd stayed, and that might've caused more trouble."

"It goes against my nature, leaving my lass to face danger without me."

"I thought you liked that I could take care of myself."

"I do."

"Look, I'm fine." Erin slid into her car and closed the door. "But Liam's not. He caught a few. He's dead."

Carlyle sighed again. "Poor blighter. I thought as much. Can you talk?"

"I'm alone."

"Any idea who did for him?"

"Not yet."

"Erin, who did you tell about this meeting?"

She felt suddenly cold. "No one. I mean, my squad knew I was meeting a CI, but I didn't say who or where. Who'd you tell?"

"Only Ian, and the lad's solid. On the other hand, I've no idea who Liam may have told, and we can't bloody well ask him now. But someone knew."

"It's got to be connected," she said.

"Or someone thinks it is. Remember, Erin, truth doesn't matter nearly as much as perception."

"And the perception's going to be that you and I got Liam killed."

He sighed a third time. "I fear you're right, lass. Mickey's not going to be happy about this."

"Are you in trouble?"

"Let me worry about Mickey."

"There's enough of him to go round. He's dangerous."

"You've no need to convince me of that, darling. I've known the lad longer than you have."

"Are you back at the Corner?"

"Aye, just arrived."

"Stay there, and keep your head down."

"That's precisely what Ian said. When the two of you agree, I'm thinking it's wise to take your advice. I'll talk to you later, darling."

Erin put the Charger in gear and wondered where to go. But she realized she already knew. Carlyle might be done talking to her, but she wasn't done with him, not yet. Dead or alive, Liam remained the best lead she had.

*   *   *

Erin parked in the police space near the Corner, hopped out, and unloaded Rolf. She turned toward the door and froze.

A woman was walking down the sidewalk not ten feet from Erin, apparently on her way into the pub. It wasn't the woman's confident walk that caught Erin's attention, or her knockout figure, or her drop-dead gorgeous face, or even her long mane of flaming red hair. It was the fact that she knew that face.

"Siobhan Finneran," Erin blurted out.

The redhead spun smoothly, with all the grace of a born dancer. When she saw Erin, her eyes narrowed. Siobhan recognized her at once.

To Erin's surprise, the moment of recognition actually seemed to relax the other woman. Siobhan had clearly been expecting something else, someone who promised more trouble than Erin could deliver.

"You're back in town," Erin said, stepping toward her.

"Was I supposed to announce myself?" Siobhan replied in her thick Irish brogue.

"Put your hands up, turn, and face the wall," Erin said, pulling her Glock.

Siobhan didn't move. "Just why would I be doing that?"

"You're under arrest."

"And just what is it I'm to have done?" Siobhan asked. If the gun in Erin's hand and the K-9 at her side made the Irishwoman nervous, she gave no sign of it.

"Murder, for starters."

"And who is it I've killed, according to you?"

"Hans Rüdel."

"Really?" Siobhan gave her a look of contemptuous disbelief. "You're accusing me of that?"

Erin stared back. The truth of the matter was complicated. It was true someone had killed Hans Rüdel, a neo-fascist terrorist, the previous year. It was also true Siobhan Finneran was an Irish assassin the O'Malleys had brought in specifically to take care of their problem with Rüdel. He'd died in a car bomb that had nearly killed Erin herself. But Erin had shot him a moment before, and he'd arguably already been dying. The evidence pointing to Siobhan was circumstantial at best. The woman had skipped town immediately after the bombing and escaped questioning. They still had a warrant out for her, but no one was expecting it to amount to anything.

The final complicating factor was that Siobhan was effectively Carlyle's adoptive daughter. Arresting her was going to screw up Erin's personal life to an unbelievable degree. But she'd gone on instinct, and she couldn't back down now.

"Face the wall, hands up," Erin said again, raising her Glock and pointing it at Siobhan. Confronted by inner turmoil, she fell back on training and experience.

"And if I don't? Are you planning on shooting me?"

"I don't *want* to," Erin replied. "But don't push me."

"Take me in if you want," Siobhan said with a beautiful, maddening smile. "I'll be out by the time you're tucked in with your night-light."

"Shut up, turn around, and face the wall," Erin snapped.

Siobhan obeyed. "Gives you a bit of a thrill, doesn't it?" she said as Erin stepped up behind her and started patting her down. "No need to be shy, love. We're hardly strangers. But you could at least buy me dinner first."

Erin was expecting to find a weapon, but she didn't. Apparently Siobhan was wise to New York's strict gun-control laws and knew better than to carry a handgun on her person when she wasn't working. All her search turned up was a roll of cash, a set of keys, a Leatherman multi-tool, an Irish passport, and a pocket cosmetic kit.

"Are we finished here?" Siobhan asked.

"Not by a long shot," Erin said, pulling out her handcuffs and slapping the bracelets on the other woman. "You have the right to remain silent..."

Siobhan seemed more amused than angered at being arrested. She wasn't even listening to the Miranda warning. On the ride back to Precinct 8, she stared out the window and hummed quietly to herself. Erin was annoyed with herself for getting annoyed. She was also irritated that she hadn't had the chance to follow up with Carlyle, but Siobhan was a potentially important catch and she wasn't about to jeopardize that.

Chapter 7

"Her again?" Webb asked. He, Vic, and Erin stood in the observation room next to the interrogation room. They were looking at Siobhan, who was sitting at the table, one arm cocked over the back of her chair, legs crossed. A small smile still played at the corners of her mouth.

"She's nothing but trouble," Vic muttered. "She lawyer up yet?"

"No," Erin said. She was perplexed by that. Siobhan was smart, and smart criminals knew to ask for an attorney right away.

"She's cocky," Webb observed. "Maybe we can use that. You think it'll help or hurt to have you in the room, O'Reilly?"

Erin shrugged. "She hates me, but that'll probably make her more talkative."

"Okay," he agreed. "You and me, then. Neshenko, stay here."

"Fine with me," Vic said. "I don't want to get any crazy on me. That woman is bat-shit."

"This has nothing to do with our case, of course," Webb said to Erin as they stepped out into the hall. "But the Rüdel homicide is still open. Let's see if we can close it."

"We'll need a confession if we want to hang it on her," Erin said. "Maybe I shouldn't have brought her in."

"We'll see," Webb said. "A lot of crooks actually want to confess. Let's hear her story, see what she's got to say for herself."

Siobhan watched them come in. Her eyes glittered when she saw Erin. She looked Webb up and down and slowly licked her lips. Erin was reminded of a cat. Not a domestic one, either. Maybe a tiger.

"Miss Finneran," Webb said, sitting down opposite her. Erin remained standing behind him, a little to one side.

"Lieutenant," she said, giving the word the British Isles pronunciation.

"What are you doing in New York City?" he asked.

"Visiting a… friend," she said, hesitating just a little before the final word.

"You flew into JFK?"

"That's what's stamped in my passport."

"You weren't detained at the airport?"

Siobhan's eyes widened in mock surprise. "Why? Am I in some sort of trouble?"

"You're on Homeland Security's list," Erin broke in. She knew, because she'd put it there. That had been one of the mopping-up details after the Civic Center bombing.

"Am I?" Siobhan replied.

That was an interesting puzzle. She should've been grabbed by the TSA as soon as she landed. But it wasn't the first time Homeland Security had screwed up and let someone fly they shouldn't have. Erin let it pass.

"We know you were gunning for Rüdel," she said. "We ran into each other looking for him, remember?"

"Excuse me," Siobhan said. "Are we talking about the lad who tried to blow up your headquarters last year?"

"You know we are," Erin said.

"The lad you shot, if memory serves?"

"That's him."

"So you're accusing me of killing the lad you were trying to kill?"

"You blew up his car," Erin said. "Innocent people could've been killed."

"You know where I come from, darling," Siobhan said with a sardonic smile. "And you know the Irish Republican Army does its best to avoid collateral casualties."

"You're saying you were careful not to blow the bomb until Rüdel was the only one in the blast zone?" Webb asked.

"You're saying that, big fella," she said. "I'm just saying, if I were to pop off a lad, I'd be careful not to hit anyone I didn't want to. I'm speaking hypothetically, of course."

"You saved my life," Erin said, looking hard at Siobhan. "You warned me about the bomb, right before it went off."

Siobhan's eyes turned hard, like chips of jade. "So now you're accusing me of assisting an officer? Would that be a crime?"

"No," Webb said. "So you warned Detective O'Reilly about the explosion?"

"Seems to me I couldn't have done that unless I'd known about the bomb ahead of time. Are you asking me to confess to something?"

Erin cursed inwardly. She and Webb had laid a trap, but Siobhan had stepped around it. Maybe the woman didn't need a lawyer after all. Siobhan was guilty, Erin knew she was guilty. Hell, Siobhan wanted them to know she was guilty. But all this was hearsay and circumstantial. None of it would lead to a conviction.

"We got DNA swabs off the bomb," Webb said suddenly.

This was a lie. Lying in interrogation was totally legal and acceptable behavior. It was also risky, because it was a bluff.

"Did you, now?" Siobhan said. "From what I heard, that's the only way you'd have been able to identify the poor bastard. It was probably all that was left of him."

"I'm talking about the bomb-maker's DNA," Webb said.

"If that's so, you'd best go arrest the lad," she retorted. "Why are you wasting my time with this conversation?"

"We know you killed him," Webb said.

"Then you'd best charge me and be done with it. We'll see how it plays out in the courts."

"Why are you here?" Erin demanded, leaning over the table toward the other woman.

"Are you codding me? You brought me here in handcuffs yourself, you bloody eejit," Siobhan snapped, her Irish coming out stronger.

"In New York, smartass," Erin said, not giving an inch. She knew an angry suspect was more likely to slip up.

"Why don't you ask your boyfriend, you feckin' floozie?"

Erin inwardly froze. Webb glanced at her, and in his eyes she saw a question he wasn't about to ask in front of a suspect. She reminded herself it would just sound like ordinary interrogation-room trash-talk to him.

"I'm asking you," she said, holding on to her self-control.

"I was wanting a drink," Siobhan said. "Or is that illegal here, too?"

"We can hold you overnight," Erin said. "Without charging you."

"If you hold me all night, it'll be a new experience for you," Siobhan said. "I expect most of your squeezes are out the door the moment they've done the job on you."

"We're done here," Webb said, standing up.

"Not quite," Siobhan said. "I'll be wanting my telephone call."

*   *   *

"What'd you think, Neshenko?" Webb asked.

Vic shrugged. "We already know she blew up Rüdel. My question is, why do we care?"

Webb gave him a hard look. "That's several major felonies we're talking about."

"So what, boss? Erin tried to kill him. I tried to kill him. Hell, you're the only guy in this room who didn't take a shot at the son of a bitch. Not her fault Erin and I only winged him."

"This isn't the Wild West, Neshenko. She's a goddamn terrorist. If she was a man and had an Arabic name, she'd be in Guantanamo Bay by now."

"Don't let the press hear you say that, sir," Vic warned.

"I'm stating a fact, not a political opinion," Webb said. He rubbed his face. "Not that we can prove any of it. We're going to have to cut her loose."

"I thought at least she'd be carrying," Erin said. "If we'd gotten her on a weapons charge, we could've held her."

"All night long," Vic said, grinning.

"In your dreams," she said, irritated. He wasn't going to let her forget Siobhan's parting shot.

"Nah, she's not my type."

"What, a gorgeous redhead doesn't light your fire?" Erin teased.

"I prefer them sane."

"Which is why you remain single. Any girl would have to be crazy to date you. It's a catch-22."

"What'd she mean about your boyfriend, anyway?" Webb asked.

Erin gave what she hoped was a nonchalant shrug. "She knows I'm in contact with Carlyle and Corcoran. I assume she meant one of them. I don't know what she meant by it."

Webb nodded. "We'll keep her for a few hours, just in case something comes up."

"We don't really have her DNA from the bombing, do we?" Erin asked.

"Nope," Webb said. "DNA from explosions is almost never any good. It's always dead cells, with environmental contamination and heat damage."

"You thought an IRA veteran wouldn't know that?" Erin asked.

"I took a chance," he said, annoyed. "You're the one who brought her in without enough evidence to charge."

Erin nodded and shut up. Webb was right.

*   *   *

The squad was back in the Major Crimes office, and Siobhan was cooling her heels in the precinct lockup. Vic was looking through file after file from the Organized Crime division, trying to make sense of the Lucarellis and where Conti had fit in. Webb was examining the little they had on Diego Rojas. Various officers came and went with bits of evidence. Erin was talking with Skip, who'd come up from his basement office.

"Forget about tracing a sale," he said. "The bomb was homemade napalm. You can mix it with ordinary stuff, off the shelf. Assuming the bomber paid cash, and wasn't dumb enough to buy all the ingredients in one place, there's no chance."

"How good was the device?" she asked.

"Wasn't much of a device. Chemical trigger, inside the bottle. They threw it, the glass shattered on impact, and boom."

"So, an amateur job?"

"I didn't say that. I'm saying a Molotov cocktail looks about the same, no matter who makes it. Hell, the whole point of them is that anyone can build one. You know how they got their name?"

Erin shook her head. Skip wasn't exactly a nerd, but on the subject of explosives he was an encyclopedia.

"Back in 1940, when the Soviet Union went to war with Finland, the Finns didn't have much in the way of weapons. After the Soviets bombed Helsinki, the Russian Foreign Minister, a guy named Molotov, said they hadn't really dropped bombs, they'd dropped bread to feed the starving people. So the Finns, dark humor specialists that they are, started calling Russian bombs 'Molotov breadbaskets.' Then, when they needed homemade anti-tank weapons, they called their gasoline bombs 'Molotov cocktails,' saying now they had a drink to go with the food."

"That's very interesting, Skip," she said, trying to keep the sarcasm out of her voice. "Are you telling me we're looking for Finnish hitmen?"

"No, I'm just telling you it could be anybody." He paused. "Including Finns, I suppose. You got any Finnish suspects?"

"It's New York City," she allowed. "Could be."

"Or it could be a professional bomb-maker," Skip added. "Like him."

"Who?" Erin asked. Then she followed his gaze past her to the stairwell. "Shit," she added under her breath.

Carlyle was standing at the entrance to Major Crimes with a man beside him who was definitely a lawyer.

"Why don't you ask him?" Skip suggested.

Erin just stared, mind racing. She had no idea what to say, but Vic took it out of her hands. He sprang to his feet and crossed the room. Erin and Rolf scrambled up and followed, Webb just a few steps behind. Vic got right in Carlyle's face.

"I think you're on the wrong floor," Vic growled. "Lockup's downstairs."

"We're on our way there now," Carlyle said, unintimidated. "But we're needing to speak with your lieutenant first."

"You want me, you got me," Webb said. "What're you doing here, Mr. Carlyle?"

"I'm here to arrange the release of one of your prisoners."

"That so?" Webb looked Carlyle over. The Irishman was immaculately dressed in a gray suit that probably cost more than Webb's entire wardrobe. He looked every inch the respectable businessman.

"Aye, that's so." He was calm, collected, and polite. But he didn't look Erin in the eye. "Miss Finneran, if you please."

"We're not required to release her at this time," Webb said.

"She's an Irish national," the lawyer said. "I'm John Walsh, and I'm representing Ms. Finneran. I have a letter here from the Irish consulate, respectfully requesting that Ms. Finneran either be charged or released at once."

"The consulate has no jurisdiction here," Vic said.

"No, sir, it doesn't," Walsh said. "But cooperation will prevent an international incident. We're requesting this as a courtesy."

Webb scanned the letter. His mouth twisted slightly, but he didn't show any other emotion. Folding it, he handed it back to the lawyer.

"O'Reilly, release our guest."

Erin cursed inwardly. "Yes, sir," she said out loud. "Gentlemen, if you'll follow me." Rolf stayed at her side.

No one said anything as she led Carlyle and his lawyer down to the holding cells. She put her Glock and her backup ankle piece in a gun locker outside the cells and went in.

Siobhan was waiting for them, reclining on an elbow on the hard bed, one long leg trailing down to the floor. She stood up when she saw them, moving with deliberate slowness, as if she had all the time in the world.

Erin unlocked the cell. "Time to go."

"Thanks for the help, Cars," Siobhan said, giving Carlyle a wide, inviting smile and ignoring Erin completely. "I knew you'd come for me."

She put her arms around his neck and drew in close, giving him a warm embrace and a kiss on the cheek. Carlyle returned the hug, then stepped back from her.

"I've a car waiting outside," he said. "Go with Mr. Walsh, please. I've a few details to clear up here."

"Don't be too long," she said, giving him a slight pout. Then she walked briskly out of the holding area. As she went, she gave Erin a quick, blazing glance which was full of triumphant hatred.

Erin followed Siobhan and Walsh out to the lobby. She and Rolf watched them go. The K-9, picking up her emotion, bristled slightly.

When she turned away from the door, Carlyle was standing there with an unreadable expression on his face. Erin glared at him.

"We need to talk," she said.

"I'm thinking we do," he replied levelly.

"C'mon," she said, motioning him to the elevator. She pushed the button for the garage. As soon as the doors opened, she grabbed him by the shoulder and pulled him off to the side, into the shadows.

"What is this?" he asked.

She glanced around. They were alone. Rolf stood warily, head slightly cocked, trying to figure out what was going on.

"There's no cameras on this part of the garage," she explained. Then she tightened her grip on him. "You come into my police station? To get *her* out?"

Carlyle grabbed her wrist and pulled her hand free of his coat. The shock of that sudden action startled Erin. He'd never laid a rough hand on her before. In that moment, seeing the look in his eyes, the tightness in his jaw, she realized he was as angry as she'd ever seen him. Rolf growled and tensed. If he had the slightest excuse, he'd jump the Irishman right there.

"That's my little girl you hauled in here," Carlyle said, biting off the words, holding on to an icy edge of control.

"She's not such a little girl," Erin retorted. "Or didn't you notice?"

"I held her hand at her da's funeral."

"She's a murderer!" Erin shot back. "You're protecting her?"

"She's my responsibility!"

"For how long? Until she does what? Where's the line?"

"When it comes to the people I love, there's no bloody line!"

She stared at him. "You don't mean that."

"I do," he said, more quietly. "I'd kill or die for them. And that goes for you too, Erin."

"You think I want that? You think that impresses me?"

"I'm not trying to impress you, Erin."

"Then what the hell are you trying to do?"

"I'm trying to do what's right!"

They stared at each other, both breathing hard. Erin wanted to punch him in the face, to shake some sense into him, to scream at him.

"So am I," she said, suddenly feeling very tired. "You picked a hell of a time to play white knight."

"I'd no choice, Erin. Why did you arrest her?"

"You know why."

"Anything she might have done, she was doing to protect this city."

"We arrest vigilantes. If goddamn Batman showed up in New York, we'd put him behind bars."

"That's beside the point. Were you looking for her today?"

"No. I came to the Corner to talk to you."

"Here I am. What is it you're wanting?"

Erin shook her head. "It wasn't supposed to go like this."

His face softened a little. "I know, and for what it's worth, I'm sorry."

"Liam knew something," she said. "And they killed him for it."

"I agree he's likely involved," Carlyle said quietly. "The lad was already nervous. It's curious, though. He agreed to meet with you. Then, when you showed up, he left almost at once."

"I guess I asked him the wrong question," she said, thinking back. "I asked him who had a reason to go after the Lucarellis. Then he freaked."

Carlyle nodded and said nothing.

"He knew the answer to that," she said softly. "That was why he got mad at you. But the only reason he would've been mad was if..."

She looked into Carlyle's face. He was putting up a careful, expressionless façade. That, by itself, answered the question she knew she couldn't ask him.

"Siobhan will be waiting for you," she said.

He straightened his jacket and adjusted his necktie. He no longer looked angry, but he was distant, cautious.

"I apologize for troubling you, Erin. I'll be leaving now."

She felt like a wall had sprung up between them, like those sheets of bulletproof glass between the telephones in prison visiting rooms. She wanted to touch him, but couldn't think how to reach him.

"I'll see you later," she said, unconvincingly.
"You know where I'll be," he replied.

Chapter 8

Erin and Rolf stepped out of the elevator into Major Crimes. Webb and Vic were at the whiteboard, conferring. They looked up in surprise.

"Get rid of the lowlifes?" Vic asked.

She ignored the question. "Liam McIntyre was behind the restaurant hit," she said.

"You sure about that?" Webb asked.

"Either he did it, or someone thinks he did," she replied.

"Carlyle tell you that?" Vic asked with an edge of contempt.

"No," she said. "He very specifically didn't tell me that."

"Which means he thinks McIntyre was involved, but doesn't want to rat out his buddies," Webb said, understanding. "So what was the hit on McIntyre? Retaliation by the Lucarellis?"

"Could be," Erin said. "They wouldn't have to know for sure. If they even thought McIntyre was involved, they might've moved on him."

"Were they tailing him, you think?" Vic asked. "They didn't just get lucky and run into him."

"Drugs," Erin said thoughtfully.

"What about them?" Webb asked.

"This whole thing was about drugs."

"Yeah, we know," Vic said. "In other news, Manhattan's an island. You wanna buy a bridge?"

"I mean, it was business, not personal," she said.

"No Godfather impressions," Webb warned Vic, who gave him a look of artificial innocence.

"Rojas was meeting with Conti to do a drug deal," Erin explained. "What if the hit was to break up the deal?"

"I think we agree that's what happened," Webb said. "We've been over this. That's why they got shot."

"But Rojas isn't dead," she said.

"Not *confirmed* dead," Webb corrected.

"Let's assume, just for a second, he's still alive," she said. "Suppose he's on his way into the meeting, but the shooting starts before he gets inside. He gets away. Now he's got a load of product to unload, but his deal fell through, his local contacts are dead, and he's lost the guys he brought with him. He's got to do something fast, or he'll have to answer to his bosses down in Colombia. Then suppose he hears from this Irish guy who says he can move some drugs."

"So Rojas murders the guy who threw him a lifeline?" Vic was skeptical.

"Not right away," Erin said. "Maybe he does the deal first. McIntyre was hopped up on something when I saw him. I wonder what the Homicide boys will find when they run his bloodwork. A few milligrams of Colombian pure, I'm guessing."

"Then what? Why kill McIntyre?" Web rubbed his chin.

She shrugged. "Paranoia. Suspicion. Or just snipping off a loose end. Liam didn't strike me as the most trustworthy, balanced guy in the world. If I were in his line, I wouldn't count on him. I'm guessing the whole thing looked just a little too convenient to a guy like Rojas."

"Pretty stupid of McIntyre," Vic said. "Whack a guy's associates, then do a deal with him right after?"

"Risky," Webb said. "Which might explain why he's on a slab right now. It's a decent theory, O'Reilly. Problem is, it's—"

"Thin," Erin and Vic chorused.

Webb gave them a sour look. "Am I that predictable?"

"Thought you might say that," Vic said.

"But you're right," Erin said. "We need proof."

"Fortunately, McIntyre's been murdered, which means we can get a warrant for his home and place of business," Webb said. "I'll put in the paperwork. You two, find out where he hangs out. If he got high before your meeting, he may have some stuff at home, even if his main stash is somewhere else."

"The Irish aren't gonna like you for this," Vic said to Erin.

"Really? That's a shame. Their approval was so very important to me."

She kept her tone light, but he was right. Evan O'Malley wasn't likely to take kindly to an investigation into his drug business.

*   *   *

Liam's home address was on Nassau Street, on the fourth floor of an old brick building with a boarded-up diner on the ground floor. Erin, Vic, and Rolf showed up with their warrant. Lawton and Crawford from Homicide met them there. Webb had stayed behind at the precinct to continue coordinating the efforts of the alphabet soup of government agencies.

"I guess it's true," Vic said, looking over the run-down apartment building. "Crime doesn't pay."

"There's plenty of money in drugs," Erin said. "Liam just put a lot of it right back up his own nose."

The building's superintendent was nowhere to be found, but Lawton had Liam's keys. While he jingled them around, trying to find the right one for the outer door, Crawford unwrapped a piece of chewing gum.

"The wife says it's better for me than cigarettes," he said, popping the stick into his mouth and chewing morosely. "But it's not the same."

"Your wife's right," Erin said.

"You smoke?" Crawford asked with a hint of hope.

"Sorry, no."

"I was a little surprised to hear from you," he went on. "Who's got jurisdiction over this mess, anyway?"

"Technically, you guys," Vic said. "We're just being good neighbors, helping you out."

"We figure anyone's inside?"

"Nope."

"But you're wearing vests," Crawford observed. "Even the dog."

"I've kicked in a lot of doors," Vic said. "Every now and then, someone shoots at me. How come you didn't tac up?"

"Guy lived alone," Crawford said. "No reason to think anyone's home. Besides," he added, looking down at himself, "I don't fit into my vest so good anymore. I blame the nicotine withdrawal. I just keep putting on weight."

"I blame the street hot dogs," Lawton said over his shoulder.

"If you guys don't have vests, we're going in first," Erin said. She'd seen one fellow officer die from an unlucky bullet and didn't want to see another go the same way.

"Fine by me," Lawton said. "Here's the key."

They went up the stairs single file, Vic in the lead, Erin and Rolf behind him, Lawton and Crawford bringing up the rear. Vic and Erin had their sidearms in hand, just in case. The stairway was narrow and smelled like cigarettes and mold. Plaster was peeling from the corner of the doorframe.

Vic paused. He glanced at Erin and cocked his head at the door, pointing silently toward it. She saw what he'd seen. The door was slightly ajar.

She nodded and wrapped her hands tighter around the grip of her Glock.

Vic kicked the door open and shouted, "NYPD! Hands in the air!"

That was as far as he got. There was a sound like a giant piece of cloth being ripped down the middle. Chunks of plaster and splinters of wood exploded into the hallway. Vic hurled himself backward, stumbling and spinning against the wall on the opposite side of the door from Erin.

The cloth-tearing sound happened again, in a shorter burst this time. Erin watched bullet holes punch through the wall, each one leaving a puff of plaster and brick dust in the air.

Some detached, clinical part of Erin's brain told her they had a shooter inside Liam's apartment, armed with an automatic weapon, probably a submachine-gun. It sounded just like the weapon that had killed Liam. Vic was still on his feet and didn't look like he'd been hit, which was good. Stepping into that doorway was probably suicidal. He was about four feet away from her and might as well be on the far side of the East River.

"Holy shit," Lawton said in a quiet, conversational tone, like he was commenting on the weather.

"Call for backup," Erin snapped at him.

"You in there!" Vic yelled. "This is the police! Drop the gun before someone gets hurt!"

The shooter's answer was another long burst of gunfire, sprayed indiscriminately through the door and into the wall. Erin dropped into a crouch, which turned out to be a good idea. Two sizable holes were punched through the wall more or less where she'd been standing. Rolf barked sharply, standing tense and ready, but there was no way she was going to send him head-on at the gunman.

Vic made eye contact with her and she knew what he was going to do. She swallowed and got ready to cover him.

The gunfire paused for a second and Vic made his move. He ducked low, leaned around the doorframe, and fired three shots from his pistol. "Cover!" he shouted. Then he lunged into the room, keeping low.

Erin followed up, moving to the other side of the doorway and thrusting the barrel of her Glock around the door. She caught a quick glimpse of movement in the corner of her eye and pivoted just in time to see a man fling himself out the window. He didn't bother to open it first, he just went, one arm in front of his face, straight through the plate glass.

Vic stood in the middle of the room, pistol dangling from one hand, mouth hanging open. Erin and Rolf had time to take two steps into the apartment before they heard the thud of the man hitting the ground, four floors down.

"Did he just do a Peter Pan?" Vic wondered aloud.

"Yeah," Erin said. She was already on her way out of the room. She squeezed passed Lawton and Crawford on the stairs. Lawton was talking to Dispatch. Crawford just looked confused.

"Where you going?" he asked as she rushed back the way they'd come.

"And *that's* why we wear vests!" she snapped, not bothering to explain herself. She took the steps two at a time, Rolf flowing down the stairs right beside her. They raced out the door and around toward the alley. Erin was expecting to find a dead body, or at best a guy with two broken legs. What she saw instead made her shake her head in silent admiration. The luckiest criminal in Manhattan had fallen four stories, blind, into an open dumpster filled with bags of something soft enough not to smash him to pulp.

She saw the torn trash bags and scattered litter where he'd landed and hauled himself out. He was obviously still able to move; there was no sign of the gunman himself. But she did see something almost as good. He hadn't made it completely unscathed. A smear of wet blood marked the side of the dumpster.

"Rolf!" Erin said.

The Shepherd immediately snapped to attention, ready for orders. She pointed to the blood and gave him his German "search" command.

"*Such!*"

The blood was still warm and the trail was very fresh. A single sniff was all it took for the K-9 to lock on to the scent. Then he was off and running. Erin kept him on leash. She didn't want him to get too far ahead, especially since she hadn't seen a gun in her quick scan of the dumpster. That meant her guy was probably still armed.

"Erin! That way!"

The shout came down from above, like an angel calling an Old Testament prophet. Or, in this case, like a Russian-American detective yelling out a fourth-story window. She glanced up and saw Vic leaning out over the alley, pointing the same way Rolf was pulling.

"In pursuit!" she called back. "We got the scent!"

"I'll call backup and secure the scene!" he replied. "Go get him!"

She'd half expected him to leap out the window and join her. It was gratifying to see Vic displaying common sense.

Rolf forged ahead, nostrils flaring, tail wagging, having the time of his life. He knew what was at stake: his favorite chew-toy as a reward. All he had to do was what he'd done a thousand times in training. He hustled around a corner toward the street. Erin just hoped the guy didn't have a car waiting for him. Rolf couldn't track a car.

But the dog didn't get all the way to the street. He stopped at a manhole cover, snuffled at it, and scratched with his front claws.

"Good boy," Erin said, crouching beside him. She could see the flakes of rust where the cover had been jimmied open and another smear of blood on the lip of the lid. She knew where the guy had gone.

But it was a tricky tactical problem. Either he'd kept running, or he was waiting at the bottom of the shaft with a gun in his hand. If she opened the hatch, she might get her head blown off. If she didn't, he might get away.

This was exactly the sort of situation a flashbang grenade would be perfect for. Unfortunately, after a few too many accidents, the NYPD didn't use them anymore. Erin had her sidearm and backup piece and that was it.

While she considered her options, a squad car pulled up outside the alley, less than ten yards from her. A pair of uniforms jumped out, probably in answer to Vic's call. They must've been right at the corner. Erin was wearing a vest that said POLICE in big white letters, but she held up her shield just in case.

"What's up, Detective?" one of the officers asked.

"Got a 10-34S," she said, giving the code for an assault in which shots had been fired. "Perp did a rabbit, I'm pretty sure he's down here." She toed the manhole cover.

"Let's go get him!" the other officer said. He was a freckle-faced kid, fresh out of the academy by the look of him.

"He still got the gun?" the older officer asked, more practical and less adventurous.

"I think so," Erin said.

"There's three of us, Sarge," the rookie insisted. "Plus the dog. We got this."

The veteran gave him a look. "And there's gonna be three of us going home at the end of the shift, kid. Plus the dog. I'm not gonna tell your mama her boy got capped on my watch. Stay away from that hole."

The kid looked disappointed but obeyed.

Erin put her mouth close to the manhole. She was pretty sure the heavy iron would stop a .45 slug. "Hey, you down there!" she shouted.

No answer.

"We know you're there!" she called. "This is the NYPD! Where do you think you're going to go? We've got thirty-five thousand officers we can call up. You can give up, or we can come get you. If we get you, and we will, you're likely to get shot. So far you haven't tagged any cops. But if you hit one of us, we're going to get mad. Let's end this day on a good note for everyone."

"Chinga tu madre."

The reply was faint but audible, and very impolite. Erin didn't speak much Spanish, but she understood that much. She also had a pretty good guess who the guy was, based on his language of choice.

"Diego Rojas," she said. "Give it up. It's over."

"You want me, perra, you come get me."

"Listen, buddy," she shot back. "You're hurt. You're stuck there. If you could run, you'd already be gone. I've got all day. Hell, I've got all week. It's going to get pretty cold and dark down there. You need medical attention. Give it up. I promise you'll get a doctor."

More officers were arriving on scene. Erin stood up from the manhole as the Patrol sergeant approached.

"What do you think?" he asked in an undertone.

"He took a swan dive from the fourth floor," she whispered back. "He's lucky he wasn't killed. No way is he running. He's hurt bad. You see his blood there?"

"Gotcha," the other officer said. "I'll call HNT."

Erin nodded. This was definitely a job for the Hostage Negotiation Team. There weren't any hostages, of course, but they were the guys to bring in to talk down a barricaded suspect. The Patrol sergeant keyed his radio and called Dispatch with the request.

"Copy," Dispatch replied. "Negotiator is en route. ETA fifteen minutes."

"We'll set up a perimeter," the sergeant said.

"Let's get some storm sewer plans," Erin suggested. "Set some officers at choke points?"

"Copy that," the sergeant said. He barked orders to the other uniforms. They quickly got organized, two pairs of patrolmen going to the nearest other sewer access points and locking down the site.

Erin was content to let their target marinate in the sewer. A little softening up would make him easier to take in. She pulled Rolf's rubber Kong ball out of her jacket pocket and tossed it to him. The K-9 snatched it out of the air, plopped to his belly, and started happily gnawing. He'd done a good job and knew it. All was right in Rolf's world.

"*Mujer policía?*"

The voice was faint, coming up from the manhole, and tight with pain.

"Yeah, I'm here," Erin said, dropping to one knee beside the shaft. "How you doing down there, Diego?"

"I want a doctor."

"We'll get you one," she said. "Where are you hurt?"

"My leg and... my cabeza."

Erin knew only a little Spanish. "Your head?"

"Si."

He was slurring his words a little and losing some of his English. Erin guessed he was going into shock.

"Hey, stay with me, Diego," she said. "Here's what I need you to do. I need you to drop your gun. I can't help you if you shoot at me, okay?"

"Hey, Detective," the Patrol sergeant muttered into her ear. "Why don't we just wait for the negotiator?"

"This guy could be dying," Erin said softly. "I don't know if he's got fifteen minutes. He sounds shocky."

"He shot at cops," the sergeant reminded her.

She nodded but didn't turn away from the manhole. The guy really didn't sound so good. "Diego?" she called more loudly. "Drop the gun. Now."

There was a faint but audible splash.

Erin took a deep breath. "Okay," she said to the officers around her. "Let's get this lid open."

The rookie came forward to lend a hand. The cover wasn't fully seated in the shaft. It was heavy but not hard to shift. Metal grated on concrete.

"You don't know what he did," the sergeant objected. He stood with four other cops, guns pointed at the open hatch. "Maybe he's got another gun."

"Diego," she called.

There was no answer.

"Diego!"

He mumbled something inaudible.

"Flashlight," Erin said to the nearest uniform. He pulled his big Maglite and extended it to her. She took it, flicked it on, and shone it down the hole, keeping her head back from the opening. Anyone looking up would see only a bright light. If Rojas was waiting to shoot at someone, there was a good chance he'd fire now.

He didn't.

Erin gave it a few seconds, then cautiously poked her head over the lip of the shaft, peering down. She saw a damp, circular hole with an iron ladder bolted to one side. A man lay crumpled at the bottom like a discarded piece of trash. She saw blood on his head. He was half-submerged in brown, filthy water. His head was sagging down. Even as she watched, he slumped sideways, his head going under the surface.

"Shit," Erin muttered. There was no time to do this by the book. She shoved her Glock into its holster and thrust the flashlight back at the man who'd given it to her.

"Keep that pointed down," she told him. "*Bleib*," she ordered Rolf, who was perfectly happy to stay with his toy. Then she went down the ladder as fast as she could without jumping onto the poor bastard at the bottom.

It was a tight fit to work her way around the wounded man's body. Erin was glad she was smaller than the average cop. She splashed into the water at the floor of the shaft, hissing at the icy cold that immediately shot up her legs. She bent down, grabbed him by the shoulders, and pulled him to a sitting position. In the light from the flashlight beam, he looked like a fresh-drowned corpse. She shook him and slapped his cheek.

"Diego!" she shouted in his face. "Come on!"

He coughed brown water and moaned.

"Good, good," she said. "Stay with me. We're gonna get you out of here." She tilted her head up and shouted, "We need a bus!"

"Already on the way," the sergeant called back.

Erin knew better than to try to move a man who'd taken a fall, especially one with a head injury. Her job was to keep him from drowning until the paramedics got there. It was crazy. He'd been shooting at her and Vic less than ten minutes earlier, and now here they were, both of them soaking wet, with her just trying to keep him alive. This was not how armed standoffs usually ended. She was already shivering. The water was near freezing and wasn't going to help Rojas's chances. He was in deep shock and rapidly going hypothermic.

Erin didn't see much choice. The best thing to do with a shock victim was to elevate the legs and lower the head, but she couldn't do that without drowning him. She carefully eased herself under him and raised his body as cautiously as possible, trying to hoist him most of the way out of the water. Then she wrapped her arms around him in a weird embrace, trying to share and conserve body heat.

They were down there for what felt like a very long time. Erin's toes and feet first throbbed, then went completely numb. But she grimly held on. She couldn't tell how badly Rojas was hurt, but he was definitely bleeding from a gash on the side of his head. The blood trickled down, staining both their coats.

"Detective!"

Erin blinked up at the flashlight. She saw a silhouette against it.

"I'm coming down!" the guy called. "I'm an EMT."

"Great," she managed to say through chattering teeth.

She'd thought it was crowded before. Now, when the burly paramedic squeezed down the shaft, it was almost impossible to move. After some awkward wriggling, she managed to get partway down the storm sewer passage and give him some room to work.

There was no way they'd get a stretcher down, of course. The paramedics worked with calm, professional skill, fitting the injured man with a cervical collar to immobilize his head, splinting his leg, and getting him rigged to a hoist. Then they winched him up the shaft. Finally, Erin tried to follow. She made it three rungs up the ladder before her legs buckled. All she could do was hold onto the ladder.

Erin hung there, too weak to climb further, too stubborn to let go. She didn't think she'd ever felt so cold in her life.

"Jesus Christ, you bunch of idiots," she heard a familiar voice growl. "Get outta my way." Then a big, strong hand snaked down under her arms and around her shoulders. She recognized the distinctive smell of Vic's aftershave. He hauled her up as if she weighed nothing, lifting her clear of the manhole.

"Vic?" she mumbled.

"Yeah?"

"What kept you?"

He grinned. "Securing the scene, just like I promised. What the hell were you doing down there?"

"Figured we needed him," she said. "Alive."

A cold, wet nose poked Erin in the ear. She turned to see Rolf's furry, anxious face. He licked her, then bent down and nosed his chew-toy toward her. He wagged his tail. It was his favorite thing in the world, he seemed to be saying, and maybe it would make his partner feel better, too.

Erin reached for her dog and rubbed his head behind the ears. "Let's get somewhere warm," she said, still shivering. "And dry."

Chapter 9

"Erin, how many times have I told you I don't want to see you during your shift?"

Sean O'Reilly Junior glared at the woman he'd never stopped thinking of as his kid sister.

"Comes with the job, Sean," she replied.

"I'm just glad you're not the one in my OR," he said, sinking into a waiting-room chair beside her.

They were at Bellevue Hospital, where the ambulance had taken Diego Rojas. Sean was a trauma surgeon. He'd just gotten done operating on the gunman.

"Don't worry about me," Erin said. They'd wanted to check her out at the hospital to be on the safe side, but she was fine once she'd changed out of her wet clothes and warmed up. Now she was wearing a set of dark blue NYPD sweats she'd had in the trunk of her Charger. She had her hands wrapped around a cup of almost-palatable hospital coffee and was feeling pretty much human again. Rolf lay beside her, taking an after-action nap.

"He's pretty banged up," Sean said. "But he'll pull through. The concussion is mild, and I don't expect any lasting neurological effects. The leg's the bad part. Compound fractures of the tibia and fibula."

"He ran half a block on that leg," Erin said.

"I'm surprised he got two steps," Sean replied. "He's a tough guy, no doubt about it. But we've pinned the bones and pumped him so full of antibiotics he'll be pissing amoxicillin. Assuming no secondary infection, he won't walk for a couple of months, but he will walk."

"No he won't," she said with a smile. "We've got him cold on attempted murder of police officers, and assuming a ballistic match on the gun we pulled out of the sewer, we have him on murder one for good measure. No way does he walk."

Sean smiled back. "Different priorities, you and me."

"Not as different as you think. I tried to save his life."

"And you did," he said, giving her shoulder a squeeze. "The shock, blood loss, and hypothermia probably would've done for him even without the drowning, if you hadn't found him. You done good, kiddo."

"When can we talk to him?" she asked.

"You better leave it overnight. His system's still pretty fragile."

"I need to know if he's got an accomplice out there," she argued. "Sean, there's a war going on. Don't take this the wrong way, but I don't want to throw you guys any more business than we have to."

"Tomorrow morning," he insisted.

A man in a black suit came into the waiting room. He scanned the room and made eye contact with Erin. They recognized one another immediately. She stood up, setting her coffee cup aside, conscious of her disheveled appearance but not really caring.

"Agent Johnson."

"Detective O'Reilly. How are you feeling?"

"I'm fine," she said, wondering where Homeland Security was getting their information. She hadn't contacted him yet.

"What's the situation with my guy?" Johnson asked.

"Excuse me, sir," Sean said, joining Erin and looking the Homeland Security guy over. "I'd like to see some ID, please."

Johnson looked at Erin, who gave him her best poker face. He shrugged and flipped open his wallet.

"Homeland Security," Sean said, whistling quietly and pretending to be impressed. "This guy a terrorist?"

"That's classified, sir," Johnson said. Erin saw the twinkle in his eye and half expected him to wink at her.

"*Our* guy," Erin said, "is recovering from surgery. We've got him in protective custody. He'll be charged in the morning."

"With what?"

"Murder, attempted murder, resisting arrest, breaking and entering, maybe some drug charges."

Johnson scratched his cheek thoughtfully. "That would not be the recommendation of Homeland Security."

Erin's jaw tightened. "He shot at cops."

"I understand that, Detective. But you have to look at the larger picture—"

"He killed a man on a Manhattan sidewalk, in broad daylight," she interrupted. "Outside a restaurant I was sitting in."

"There's bigger fish he can—" Johnson started to say.

"He sprayed automatic gunfire on a busy street," she countered.

"I'm just saying, if I could talk to him—"

"I froze my ass off holding his dead weight out of the water in a damn storm sewer," she snapped. "You can have your time with him once we're done with him. Once he's charged."

Johnson's teeth grated on each other. "I've been impressed with our interagency cooperation in the past, Detective," he said quietly. "I'd be disappointed if that pattern didn't continue. I'll talk to my superiors and tell them the NYPD has the situation in hand. I assume you'll reciprocate by keeping me apprised of any future developments?"

"Copy that," Erin said.

"You think maybe you were a little hard on him?" Sean asked after the Homeland Security guy had left.

"He wants to turn that jerk loose," she said. "After what he did!"

"He didn't say that."

"Read between the lines!" she snapped. "He wants to offer Rojas a deal. We don't cut deals with murderers. Not in my town!"

Sean grinned. "You know what they say in *The Godfather*, right?"

She gave him a suspicious look.

"This is business, Erin," he said, doing his best James Caan impression. "This is business, and you're takin' it very personal."

"You know what else they say in that movie?" she retorted. This was the second time she'd had that movie line thrown at her that week, and she was sick of it. "You're my brother, and I love you, but don't ever take sides against the family."

He laughed. "Okay, Don Erin. But if you hate this guy Rojas so much, why'd you go down a sewer drain to save him?"

"You're one to talk. You stuck his leg back together."

"That's my job, Erin."

"Mine, too."

"But you still want to lock him up."

"That's different."

He looked at her. "Yeah, maybe it is. You know what? Maybe you'd better talk to Rojas now, after all."

Erin was surprised. "What? But you said..."

"I know what I said. But who knows what this Homeland guy will come up with overnight? You've got to take it easy on him, though. And one condition: I've got to be in the room while you're talking to him."

"To make sure I don't beat a confession out of him?" she suggested, half joking.

"To make sure he doesn't go back into shock and die," Sean replied, not joking at all.

*   *   *

Rojas lay in the hospital bed, a bandage swaddling his head, an IV line in his arm, a rigid cast on his leg. A handcuff secured one wrist to the bedframe. The usual array of beeping medical machinery kept time with the slow rise and fall of his chest.

He watched Erin's approach through half-open eyes. She came to a stop a couple of steps away and looked down at him, wondering how clear-headed he'd be.

"*Buenos dias, senora,*" he said. "I have seen you before, I think."

"How are you feeling, Mr. Rojas?" she asked.

His lip curled into a slight hint of a smile. "I have been worse. What do you want?"

Erin considered the man. Sean was right. He was a tough guy, for sure, Colombian cartel muscle. There was absolutely nothing she could threaten him with that his employer couldn't go one better. He might be buyable, and he might not. What approach might work best?

"What do *you* want?" she echoed.

"Nothing you can give me."

Erin saw a chair in the corner. She pulled it over and took a seat close to the bed, staying just out of arm's reach. He was weak and injured, but that was no reason to be careless.

"Mr. Rojas, I know why you're here," she said. "You got screwed, buddy. You came up to New York to do some business, and it didn't go the way it was supposed to. I know who screwed you, too. I know about Liam, and the drugs."

She was guessing, but she knew they were good guesses. One of the best ways to get suspects to give up information was to make them think you already had the answers.

Rojas said nothing. He was watching Erin from under his eyelids, measuring her. All interrogations were two-way streets. What was he learning from her?

"You can't go back to Colombia," she said.

He gave his slight smile again. "You think I am stupid?" He rattled the handcuff against the bed rail. "I am not going anywhere."

"That's not what I mean." Erin took out her cuff key. They weren't her handcuffs, but that didn't matter. Police cuffs had universal keys. She leaned in and unlocked the cuffs. She was ready if he tried anything, but Rojas didn't move. He kept watching her, confused now. That was good. Confused criminals let things slip.

"We're not the guys you need to worry about," she said. "You lost your shipment, the guys you came with are all dead. Hell, your bosses just might think you stole the goods yourself, since you're the only one still standing."

She saw the reaction in Rojas's eyes and knew she was right. She wasn't saying anything he hadn't already thought. This guy was no idiot. The cartels had a very low tolerance for failure and none whatsoever for betrayal.

"So what are you offering, *senora*? You give me protection?" He gave a short bark of a laugh.

"Nope," Erin said. She had a guess what he did want. Oddly, manipulating him to help her actually required telling him the truth. "We got a guy who's going to come in here tomorrow morning and offer you a pretty sweet deal."

"Why are you here now, if that is true?" Rojas was definitely confused now.

"He'll offer you government protection, hell, maybe full immunity. He'll want information about your bosses. But as long as you cough that up, you can pretty much write your own ticket."

"I will tell you nothing about my employers. And I will tell him nothing."

Erin nodded. She'd expected as much. He was a good soldier, loyal, dedicated. "I don't give a shit about your employers."

"I do not understand."

She made eye contact with him, drawing on everything she'd learned from all her time with Carlyle and his associates. "You're in deep trouble, Rojas. Your only way out is to take care of the guys who screwed you, and to get your product back. That'll prove your loyalty. But you've got two problems. We've got you, and you've got a bad leg, so you aren't going to be chasing anybody, even if you get out of the hospital."

"What are you saying?" Rojas asked.

Erin leaned forward, speaking low and quietly. "These bastards shot up a restaurant. They didn't just kill your people, they killed innocent bystanders. My boss wants them, as much as you do. I know Liam was one of them. But so do you. Tell me who the others are."

"You think I know them?"

"I think you know something. Names, faces, something. You knew where Liam lived."

Rojas was smiling again. "I am good at my job."

"I know," she said. "Help me finish it for you."

"Why? What do I get from you?"

"You? Nothing." Erin smiled at him, trying to remember the cold, icy way Evan O'Malley smiled, all teeth, no soul. "Except revenge."

"You are an unusual *mujer policía*," he said. "First you shoot at me, then you save my life, now you want to help me?"

She shrugged. "You've got a job to do. So do I."

Rojas lay back, staring at the ceiling. "The *policía* at home, they belong to the cartels," he said. "They always want money. You want money? A percentage?"

"Bribing a New York cop is a felony," she said.

"So you will do this, without money? The Colombian *policía* are smarter than you, I think." Rojas chuckled weakly.

"Maybe," she said. "But it's easier on your bottom line."

"He comes to me," Rojas said. "He knows the hotel I am at. He calls me, tells me to meet him, that he can give good price for an import of... coffee."

"Right," Erin said, understanding.

"I know he is the one who stopped the first meeting."

"How'd you know?"

Rojas gave her a look. "How do you think? He knows where I am. He knows what I have. He knows I have no more buyer."

Erin nodded.

"I would never go to a meeting like he said," Rojas said. "They would kill me and take what they wanted. I say okay, I will meet with him. I go to the place, very careful, watching. I see him, and four of his people. I creep out of my car, get close, see their faces. They wait for me, fifteen, thirty minutes past the meeting time. Then they go. I go to follow them, but you know what happens?"

"What?"

Rojas's smile was bitterly amused. "They steal my car."

"What?" Erin repeated.

"My car," he said patiently. "It is not where I put it. He has another man, I think. Stupid of me. I have the same car as before, they know what it looks like, they take it while I wait. The buyer, he takes a call on his phone and then leaves the meeting. The call is from the *puta* who stole my car."

"And the product was in the car," Erin said.

"*Si*," Rojas sighed. Then he winced in pain.

"So what did you do?" she pressed.

"I call a taxi," he said. "I tell him to drive the way the buyer went. I see my car, outside his apartment. I get out and watch the place, very careful. But he goes again, while I watch. I follow him. He goes to a restaurant and goes inside. I think he will be there a little while. But he comes out very fast, only a few minutes, and sees me."

"So you shot him."

Rojas wasn't going to confess straight-up to murder, no matter what Erin said to him. "He sees me, that is the end of it," he said. "So I go to his apartment, to get my product back."

"There wasn't anything in the apartment," she said. Vic and the two Homicide detectives would've certainly noticed bags full of heroin, and the CSU team was going over the place with a fine-toothed comb.

"There is a picture," Rojas said. He was breathing more rapidly now. Sweat beaded his forehead.

"A picture?" she repeated, not sure she'd heard him correctly.

"In the bedroom," he said. "A photograph. The men, the other ones, the ones who kill my people, they are in this photograph."

"Is the picture still there?" Erin asked, excitement surging up in her.

"*Si*," he said.

He'd had to drop the photo in order to shoot at her and Vic, Erin thought sourly. But that meant the picture was still in Liam's bedroom, probably lying on the floor. That might be enough to ID the shooters.

"You're sure they were the same guys?"

He nodded. "I am sure." Then he sagged into his pillow with a groan. His face was pale and sweat was running down his cheeks.

"Erin," Sean said, coming forward from the doorway. "You're going to have to stop. He needs to rest now."

"Okay," she said reluctantly, standing up. It wasn't much, but it was more than she'd had. Before she left, she refastened the handcuff to the bed rail. Rojas didn't seem to care, or even to notice.

"Thanks, Sean," she said, going on tiptoes to plant a kiss on her brother's cheek on the way out. "I've got to run."

"Of course you do," he said. "Be safe. Y'know, you're better at this police stuff than I thought. I didn't think a guy like that would say anything. Dad would be proud."

*   *   *

Erin called Vic from her car. "What're you doing?" she asked.

"Sitting in my skivvies, drinking vodka straight from the bottle and cleaning my guns."

"I asked what you're doing, not what you want to be doing."

"Oh. Cataloguing evidence."

"That's what I hoped. You back at the Eightball?"

"Yeah. How's our shooter?"

"He'll pull through. I've got a question."

"I got all kinds of answers. Want to see if one of them's the right one?"

"Did CSU find a photograph in the bedroom? It'd be lying loose, maybe on the floor."

"Just a sec." Erin heard Vic rummaging in the evidence bags. "Yeah, here it is. CSU dusted it for prints, we got a good thumbprint on the front and a couple partials on the back. Probably a match with our suspect. Not that we're really in any doubt he's our guy, but every little bit helps, right?"

"Who's in the picture?" she asked.

"Looks like a snap of some guys at a bar. Hang on, I'll take a shot on my phone and send it to you." There was a brief pause. "Can't figure out how to do it while we're still on the line. You want to tell me what you're looking for before I hang up?"

"Trying to ID the guys in the picture," she explained. "Rojas says they're our shooters from the restaurant hit."

"Really?" Vic sounded more interested. Erin could picture him turning the photo over in his hands and looking at it.

There was a pause.

"Erin..."

She knew from his voice something was wrong. She hated playing guessing games over the phone. "What?" she demanded.

"You sure this is the one he meant?"

"How the hell am I supposed to know that? He said he found a picture in McIntyre's bedroom that had McIntyre's guys in it, and he thinks they're the ones who helped him hit the restaurant."

"Okay," Vic said, uncharacteristically subdued. "I'll send it right away. You coming back to the precinct?"

"That's the plan."

"Okay," he said again and hung up.

"What was that all about?" she asked Rolf.

He wagged his tail hesitantly. He didn't know.

Erin's phone buzzed with Vic's incoming text. She opened it and saw the photo he'd attached. She poked it with a finger to expand the image.

The bottom dropped out of her stomach. She knew the bar in the photograph. And she knew some of the men in the picture.

"Son of a bitch," she muttered.

The bar was as familiar to her as her own living room. It was the Barley Corner. The picture was of one of the big tables in the middle of the room. Liam McIntyre was sitting with five other men. She didn't know three of them, but the other two had faces she was never likely to forget.

James Corcoran grinned at the camera, eyes sparkling with his customary roguish good humor. He had an arm around the shoulder of his best mate and childhood friend. Morton Carlyle wasn't smiling. He seemed to be looking straight into Erin's eyes, an unreadable expression on his face.

"Son of a bitch," Erin repeated. She sank back into the Charger's upholstery and closed her eyes. What the hell was she supposed to do now?

At least Vic didn't know about her relationship with Carlyle. He just thought the Irishman was Erin's CI. But he did know they had a history. How much more was he guessing? She tried to remember exactly how he'd sounded. How sure was she that Vic didn't know? And he wasn't the only one she had to worry about. Kira Jones, one of Erin's best friends at Precinct 8, knew at least a little. And Kira was working for Internal Affairs now.

She had a choice to make, and no option felt right. The photograph was a genuine lead. If she didn't follow up on it, they might not crack the case. And the very fact that she was thinking that way was worrisome.

"What would you do, boy?" she asked Rolf.

He stared at her. His answer was obvious.

"You'd go after the bad guys," she said. "Of course."

She put the Charger in gear. It was time to move. But she wasn't going back to the Precinct; not yet. She had to see someone first. It wasn't protocol, it might not even be smart, but she had to do it.

Chapter 10

"Good afternoon." Carlyle's voice on the phone was wary. "To what do I owe the pleasure?"

Erin hadn't wanted to make this call. She didn't even know where the two of them stood after their previous confrontation. But what choice was there?

"I need to see you," she said. "Alone."

"When?"

"Right away."

"Where?"

"My place, if you can make sure you're not followed."

"Who's to be following me? Your people, or mine?"

"Both. Plus maybe some Italians and Colombians. Be careful; they may be hunting you."

"I see. Give me a few minutes to get things in order. I can be there in half an hour."

"Thanks." She wanted to say something else, but didn't know what. She lamely ended with, "See you."

*   *   *

Erin didn't call Webb yet. She should have told him where she was and what she was doing, but she honestly wasn't sure what to tell him. Instead, she drove to her apartment, parked in the garage, and went upstairs with Rolf to wait for her boyfriend.

Carlyle was nothing if not punctual. Precisely half an hour after their phone call, he buzzed the building's front door. Erin knew he could bypass the external security, but he was respecting the boundary. She wondered what that meant. Every word, every gesture he made had some specific, deliberate meaning. She let him in. A few moments later, he rang her doorbell.

There he was in the hallway, neatly dressed as ever, tie perfectly knotted. He seemed calm on the outside, but she knew him well enough to recognize the hidden tension in his posture. His hands were empty, one clasping the other at his belt buckle.

She opened the door. "Thanks for coming," she said.

"Always."

"C'mon in."

He stepped inside. Rolf, standing in the kitchen doorway, bristled slightly. He hadn't forgotten his partner's last encounter with the Irishman. The Shepherd's baleful stare followed Carlyle into the living room.

"Have a seat," she said.

He hesitated. "Is this official?"

"I don't know."

Carlyle cocked his head. "That's the one answer I wasn't expecting." He slowly sat on Erin's couch, resting his hands on his knees. "I'm assuming you're still angry with me."

Erin nodded, tight-lipped. "Yeah. But this isn't about that."

"How may I help you, then?"

"Liam wasn't your friend."

Carlyle shook his head.

"We got the guy who killed him," she said.

"Grand. My congratulations."

Erin watched him carefully. Carlyle gave nothing away. He was watching her in return, searching her face for some clue. All interrogations were two-way, she thought for the second time that day.

"The Colombians and Lucarellis were killed by Irish," she said flatly.

Carlyle didn't flinch. "You're certain of this?" he asked quietly.

"Doesn't really matter how certain I am," she shot back. "What matters is the Colombians are sure."

"There were survivors?"

"Did Liam have a line on a big shipment of heroin?" she asked, ignoring his question.

"I've nothing to do with narcotics, Erin. You know that."

"What do your pals say?"

"I've no friends in the narcotics business, either."

"Your business associates, then."

"Erin, don't ask me about O'Malley business."

"Because you won't rat out your comrades?"

"Because I've no interest in being murdered."

"These bastards don't deserve your loyalty."

"It's not about deserving it," he said. "It's about my own integrity."

Erin wanted to smack him. Instead, she took out her phone, turned on the screen, and shoved it across the coffee table. "Who's in the picture?" she demanded.

Carlyle looked at it. "Corky, Liam, and myself," he said.

"Who else?" she growled. Both of them knew perfectly well he was only identifying guys she already knew.

"I really can't say."

"We'll get these guys through facial recognition," she said.

"Then you've no need of my testimony." He pushed the phone back toward her.

Erin came around the table and sat on the other end of the couch, angled toward him. "Look, Carlyle, this isn't what I want to be doing. This thing, you and me, it's not supposed to be about crap like this. But this case is big. We've got eleven bodies and counting. *Eleven.* And you're sitting over there doing your cool cucumber act, like it doesn't have anything to do with you. Thing is, Diego Rojas is sure Liam and his guys did the shooting. And I can't walk away just because it's O'Malley muscle in the spotlight. Do you know what sort of spot this puts me in?"

He nodded and his face and posture softened a little. "About the same spot I'm in on account of making time with a fair copper. You knew this might happen when you threw in with me."

"You don't even like these guys!" she burst out.

"As I recall, you had some difficulties with a couple of shamuses back in Queens, aye?"

Erin thought of Lyons and Spinelli, the two Homicide jerks who'd gotten her suspended from duty. "Yeah?" she said suspiciously.

"If the pair of them got in trouble through doing something thick and called for help, would you be sitting it out? Or would you be running to the rescue?"

"I'd back them up," she said.

"Why?"

"Because that's what we do."

"Precisely."

Erin sighed. "I just wanted... to work together on this. We work well as partners."

"Aye, we do."

"This photo's evidence," she went on, indicating her phone. "It's already logged. I have to report what Rojas told me. That'll make you at least a person of interest, maybe a suspect. Corky, too."

"Erin," he said.

"Yeah?"

"I'd nothing to do with the hit. I knew nothing about it. Neither did Corky."

She believed him. Part of it was the trust they'd built up so slowly and carefully over the past months. Part of it was knowing Carlyle wasn't on the muscle side of the O'Malleys. And part of it was knowing he was a pretty lousy shot and didn't like guns. That was why he kept guys like Ian around.

Guys like Ian...

She felt suddenly cold. They were looking for four shooters. Three had blasted the front of the restaurant, the fourth had waited out back and gunned down the Italians as they'd fled. The last one had been an expert marksman, dealing out perfect head shots. Exactly the sort of shots a Marine Scout Sniper knew how to make.

"Erin?" Carlyle asked, leaning toward her. "What's the matter? You look like you've just taken a shot to the belly."

"I'm fine," she said mechanically.

"Erin," he said again. "I didn't do this."

"I know."

"For what it's worth, I'm sorry about Siobhan."

She nodded, but she was thinking about other things. "Carlyle," she said slowly, "is there any chance any of your people might be working... for someone else? Do you, I don't know, rent them out or something? As a favor, ever?"

"You mean, do I think any of my folk were moonlighting for Liam? It's possible. But if so, they've not told me. People in the Life are always looking for a way to get ahead, as you well know. It's not like we sign exclusive contracts."

That startled a smile out of her. "But these guys in the picture," she said, tapping her phone. "They're not yours? They don't answer to you?"

"They don't," he confirmed.

"But you won't tell me anything else about them."

"I'd like to help you." His face became even more intent. "How important is it to you?"

"I'm going to find out," she promised. "One way or another, with your help or without it."

"That's no answer."

"A guy I know taught me how not to answer questions."

It was his turn to smile. "I love you, darling," he said. "There's not much I'd not do for you. But if we start down this road, it could well lead to a funeral, or more than one. Is it worth it?"

"I need to trust you," she said, without thinking. And just like that, there it was. The heart of the matter.

He sat back. "Ah," he said quietly.

"If I can't, this is never going to work," she said.

"We've fought side by side," he reminded her.

"But we're not on the same side."

"I'm no copper," he said. "But I'm not like the rest of them, either."

"Prove it."

"Erin, if you take O'Malley lads down for this, I'm not sure I can square it with Evan."

"I'm not scared of him," she said, almost truthfully.

"Oh, he'll not likely move directly against you," Carlyle said. "That's not my concern. But if this tells him you're outside my control, he'll see no use in you. Then, if I keep seeing you, he'll know you're a liability, which means I am, too."

"So he won't trust you?"

He gave her a wry smile. "You think he trusts me now? Evan O'Malley doesn't trust anyone, Erin. But he finds me useful. The moment he doesn't, I'm done."

"Done, as in..."

"Done," he repeated.

"If Evan does decide you're a liability," she said, "how will you know?"

"I'll know when the bullet goes into the back of my head. He'll use someone close to me, so I'll not see it coming."

"Someone like Corky or Ian?"

"Anyone but them," he said. "Corky's the one lad who'd never betray me, and Ian's... well, he's a special case. He's not, precisely, in the Life."

"You can't be a part-time gangster," Erin said.

Carlyle laughed quietly. "Ian always wanted to be one of the lads, but I wouldn't let him. I helped him through school, kept him out of trouble with the coppers. You've seen his file, I'm sure."

She nodded.

"Then you know the lad's been clean for better than ten years. I'd like to think I put him on a better path."

"Then why's he still here? Why's he working for you?"

"The poor lad had some rough experiences overseas, with the Marines. I fear combat left him with a particular set of skills and a mindset not well-suited to most employment."

"In other words, he's a professional killer," she said.

"If he is, it's your government made him one," Carlyle said sharply. "He'd kill for me if he had to, but he's never done it."

"He's another one of yours," Erin said softly, understanding.

He raised an eyebrow. "Would you care to elaborate?"

"Siobhan's like a daughter to you," she said. "Ian's like a son."

"Maybe."

"You really want a family, don't you," she said. It was more statement than question.

"Erin, you're from a stable home," he said. "I'll wager you've always wanted to impress your da, but you never really worried about losing your parents' love, did you?"

"Of course not," she said. "Dad might've kicked my ass if I screwed up, but he'd never stop loving me."

"The British killed my da when I was just a lad. And my mum always preferred Norbert."

Erin knew Carlyle was talking about his brother. They hadn't spoken since Carlyle had left Ireland nineteen years earlier.

"When I found Rose, I thought maybe I'd a chance at my own family," he went on. "But those UVF bastards got her, and there was an end to it. Family? You take it for granted, Erin. You with your warmhearted mum, and your da who's so proud of you. I know how the world can strip away everything a man loves, so he's got to fight for it. I'll not be letting anyone take the ones I love from me, not while I'm standing. Do you understand?"

Erin nodded. "I do." She felt a sudden tenderness toward this complicated, careful man. Without thought or plan, she reached out and took his hand.

"It's a weakness, in my line of work," he said. "Caring about anyone. And I've no doubt it'll get me, in the end. But I've no regrets."

"I do love you," she blurted out.

He blinked and smiled sadly. "Aye, darling. I know it. That's what makes this so bloody hard on the both of us."

"So what happens now?"

Carlyle sighed. "Let me see the picture again."

Erin wordlessly opened the image and handed her phone to him.

"Pat Maginty, Lonnie Burke, and Twitchy Newton."

"Twitchy?" she echoed.

"I don't know his right name. Everyone calls him that."

"Thanks," she said. "I mean it."

"Don't thank me, Erin." His face was grim. "This will likely mean trouble for the both of us down the road."

"Can you tell me anything else about them?"

"Nothing you'll not find in your files." He stood up. "I'd best be getting back. Ian's got the car out front."

She got up and laid a hand on his arm. "Be careful, okay?"

"I'm always careful."

"Extra careful, then. Watch everybody. Especially the people you trust."

"Erin?" he said. "Do you know something?"

"Nothing certain. Just watch your back, okay? And your front, while you're at it."

"You do the same, darling."

"My people aren't as likely to murder me."

"All the same."

"Carlyle?"

"Aye?"

"Are we good?"

He smiled then, and for a moment the worry left his face. "Aye, we're grand, you and I. No fear, we'll figure something. I'll be seeing you, darling."

He bent down, aiming a kiss at her cheek. On an impulse, she turned so she met him with her lips on his. He let the kiss linger a moment before he drew back, surprised but pleased.

When the door closed behind him, she went to her window and looked out. Two floors down, Carlyle's dark gray Mercedes idled on the street. She saw Ian Thompson get out of the driver's seat. The former Marine looked both ways, then opened the car door for his boss. Carlyle got in. Ian climbed back behind the wheel and drove away. She watched them go and wondered.

Chapter 11

"I've got names," Erin announced by way of a greeting.

"Our shooters?" Webb asked, looking up from his desk.

"Yeah."

"You take lessons from that magician we busted?" Vic asked. "Got a rabbit you pulled out of a hat?"

"I don't care if it's magic," Webb said. "I care about results. Who are they?"

"Three Irish guys," she said, going to the whiteboard and picking up a marker. "Pat Maginty, Lonnie Burke, and Twitchy Newton."

"How good is this info?" Webb asked.

"They're the men in a photo from McIntyre's apartment," she explained. "Vic's got the picture."

"They're not all the guys in that pic," Vic said. "We got a couple of old friends there, too."

"Corcoran and Carlyle weren't shooters," she said. "Hell, neither of them even carries a gun."

"Carlyle?" Webb said sharply. "Our buddy the bar owner?"

"Yeah," she said wearily.

"Who gave you the names?" he asked.

"A CI."

"One affiliated with the O'Malleys?"

"I don't want to reveal anything about him," she said.

"Our good friend Anonymous comes through again," Vic said. "Best source the department has."

"Anyway, Rojas was positive he recognized the guys in that pic as men McIntyre had with him," Erin said. "Rojas is sure McIntyre shot up his deal, ripped off his heroin, and tried to screw him again on the re-sell."

"And that's why Rojas popped McIntyre," Webb said.

"He's a murderous asshole," Vic said. "But at least his motive's understandable. Crooks hate getting robbed. It's ironic, don't you think?"

"Ironic or not, it's the best lead we've got," Webb said. "Take these names and see what you can find. I'll shoot them over to Johnson at Homeland Security and see if he's got anything. As long as we've got the Feds breathing down our necks, we might as well get some use out of them."

Erin looked up Pat Maginty and Twitchy Newton. Unsurprisingly, both of them had fat files with the NYPD. Maginty was an O'Malley enforcer with a long string of drug, weapons, and assault charges. He'd spent half his life in jail and the other half doing the things that had landed him there. He'd just gotten out of Riker's Island four months ago, after serving eighteen months for aggravated assault. Apparently he'd gotten upset at a café, jumped the counter, and bludgeoned another patron with a hot waffle iron of all things. According to the police report, it had left some unique scars.

Newton was cut from the same mold. His real name was Timothy. The "Twitchy" handle had stuck after his first major felony conviction. He'd been robbing a payday loan joint, practiced poor trigger discipline, and accidentally fired a revolver twice into the ceiling and once into the leg of an accomplice. That little stunt had landed him five years. Erin was surprised he hadn't gone down longer for armed robbery; five years was the minimum sentencing. She guessed the judge had thought he was as much a danger to his fellow criminals and himself as to law-abiding society. He'd been in and out of prison ever since.

She and Vic compared notes and found more depressing similarities. Burke was suspected in a double homicide, but the charges hadn't stuck.

"Lack of evidence," Vic said. "They never found the murder weapon, and the eyewitness had a change of heart. Standard organized-crime dead end. God, I hate mob hits. What do you think?"

"I think they could be our guys," she said. "They've sure got the pedigree."

"Yeah," he agreed. "But we don't have evidence on them."

"But we can do surveillance," she said. "Maybe get warrants for their phones, check their cars, see if we can find something."

"They'll have got rid of the guns already," he said. "But McIntyre getting popped probably rattled them. They'll either spook or go to ground."

"I've got addresses for Newton and Maginty," she said. "Through their parole records."

"Same for my guy," Vic said. "It's a start."

When they showed Webb what they had, he agreed. He'd just gotten off the phone with Homeland Security, but that hadn't done any good.

"They're not on any watch lists," he said. "The only O'Malley guys the Feds have on their radar are former IRA associates: your buddies Carlyle and Corcoran, the Finneran girl, and some guy called Pritchard who's in Jersey as far as they know. As far as they're concerned, the rest of them are just garden-variety thugs. By the way, Homeland Security apologizes about

Finneran slipping through. Apparently, she got misfiled somehow. Could be corruption or could be garden-variety institutional incompetence. Hard to tell with the Feds.

"Anyway, we've got some extra NYPD bodies to throw at this, so I'll get the Captain to give us some plainclothes guys. We'll stick them on all three of these mopes and see where they lead us. In the meantime, draw up some warrants and we'll see if we can get Judge Ferris to sign off for home searches. Shouldn't be too hard. They're all on parole or probation right now."

"Whoa," Vic said, nudging Erin. "Look what just wandered in."

Kira Jones was standing in the stairwell, hesitating. She put one foot into Major Crimes, paused again, and made eye contact with Erin.

"Hey, stranger," Erin said.

"Hey, Erin."

"Whatcha doin' here?" Vic asked. "Decided to do some police work for a change?" He hadn't forgiven Kira for transferring out of their squad into Internal Affairs.

"I need to talk to you," Kira said to Erin. "Well, not me. My boss."

"Lieutenant Keane?" Erin asked.

"Yeah. Can you step upstairs for a minute? It shouldn't take long. You're not in trouble or anything."

"Just what I needed to make my day complete," she muttered. "Okay, Rolf. *Komm*."

"Don't worry, Erin," Vic said behind her. "Internal Affairs says you're not in trouble. Don't you feel better knowing that?"

*   *   *

Erin didn't like Lieutenant Keane, but that wasn't unusual. As far as she knew, no one liked him. That was fine with

"Bloodhound" Keane. The head of an Internal Affairs office wasn't supposed to be popular. He was the youngest lieutenant in the NYPD: smart, ambitious, and completely ruthless. And Erin knew he'd gotten her the gold shield she wore, saving her career in the process.

She didn't like owing favors to anyone, no matter which side of the law they were on. So, she gritted her teeth on her way upstairs and tried to think what Keane could possibly want with her. The one thing she was sure of was that a call from IAB was never, ever good news.

Kira didn't offer any information on the way up, and Erin couldn't think of anything to say to her. Rolf padded beside her, a warm, solid support. Erin was grateful for his presence.

On the third floor, Kira peeled off to her desk, leaving Erin and Rolf to walk the last few yards to Keane's office unescorted. His door was closed. She took a breath and knocked.

"Come in."

Keane was seated behind his desk, a sharp-faced man, perfectly dressed, clean-shaven, every hair combed exactly right. He had a thin hint of a smile at one corner of his mouth that looked slightly mocking.

"Detective O'Reilly," he said. "Thanks for coming so quickly. I'm glad Kira caught you in the office. Please close the door and have a seat."

Erin sat down without saying anything. She was certain Keane had known exactly where she was before he'd sent Kira down.

"I see you've still got your K-9 with you," he went on. "I was just reading over the arrest report for Diego Rojas. Fine work, Detective. From the sound of it, it's a good thing you've got your dog on your squad, or he might have slipped away."

"He'd be dead if he had," she said. "They almost lost him on the way to the hospital. If he hadn't gotten medical attention, he'd be done."

"But then you wouldn't have gotten any further leads." He leaned forward slightly. "I don't need to remind you, there's a lot of attention being focused on this case, all the way from the top."

Erin nodded.

"It'll be a real feather in your cap if you collar the surviving gunmen," he said. "Am I right in assuming Liam McIntyre was one of them?"

"We don't know if he actually fired any shots," she said. "But we're pretty sure he masterminded the attack. He might've been there, he might not."

"But you can't arrest him, more's the pity," Keane said, leaning back in his chair again. "Was he already a suspect when you met with him, right before he was shot?"

Danger signals went off in the back of Erin's mind. "No," she said, choosing her words carefully. She couldn't let Keane, of all people, suspect the real nature of her relationship with Carlyle and the O'Malleys. "I was using him as an informant, looking for background on drug operations. I knew he was competition for the Lucarellis, so I thought he might be willing to tell me something about them we could use."

"Was he helpful?"

"No. He got spooked and left, just in time to get mowed down."

Keane's smile grew wider. "I see. Well, I imagine it's just a matter of mopping up now. With Rojas in custody, all you need to do is sweep up what's left of McIntyre's crew. You know who you're looking for?"

"Yeah."

"Can you tie them to the hit?"

"Not yet. But we're getting warrants. There's a chance at least one of them will have something. Then we can lean on that guy to break them open. We're confident we've got the right guys."

"Good."

"Sir?"

Keane raised a polite eyebrow. "Yes?"

"Why am I here?" She knew it wasn't a good idea to ask a question like that. The best way to be around Internal Affairs was quiet. Erin was from a police family. She knew all about the Blue Wall. Cops protected other cops. It was way too easy to screw up procedures; every officer lived in a state of mild infraction at best, and the only hope was not to get jammed up too badly.

"Do you have any ideas on the subject of why I might want to talk to you?" Keane asked. His smile was still wide, almost predatory.

Erin thought back to the card game Carlyle had invited her to at his place back in February, a gathering of the O'Malley leadership. She'd stonewalled scarier guys than Keane. He wasn't going to shake her with a simple question like that. She cocked her head at him the way Rolf did when he was trying to figure what was going on.

Seconds ticked by. Erin didn't move, didn't speak, didn't flinch. She tried to put an expression of polite interest on her face.

"There have been some concerns," Keane said at last. "My office is aware that you've formed an association with one or more members of the O'Malleys. You can understand why that might be of interest to the department?"

Erin shrugged. "I'm a detective. We talk to a lot of shady characters. I've gotten some good intel from a couple of sources in that organization."

He nodded. "Which ones?"

"I'm not at liberty to discuss that, sir," she said. "For obvious reasons, informants' names can't be freely passed around, even among police. The CI's life would be in danger if a name got mentioned, even in your office. I'm sure you understand, sir."

"Of course," Keane said. "Well, I appreciate that you're being careful, Detective. I understand some of the ethical gray areas an officer can get into. If you should happen to find yourself in a... difficult situation, I hope you know you can come to me. I have some experience in extricating officers from unforeseen complications."

"I'll keep that in mind, sir."

Keane stood up. "Thank you for your time, Detective. That will be all."

Erin got to her feet, puzzled. That was it? She wanted to say something but knew it would be a terrible idea. Instead, she shook hands with the Lieutenant, got hold of Rolf's leash, and left the office.

Outside, Kira shot her a sidelong look and spread her hands in a gesture that was a clear question: *how did it go?*

Erin gave her a small shrug by way of answer. Then she went down to Major Crimes to get back to work.

*   *   *

The warrants were waiting when she got there. Under Article 700 of New York's Criminal Procedure Law, the NYPD needed the proper paperwork to start eavesdropping and video surveillance. Now they could tap phones, peek through windows, and do all the creepy Big Brother spying they could imagine. They also had search warrants, but Webb wasn't keen on serving those just yet.

"It's better to keep them in the dark," he said. "Assuming these guys aren't complete morons, they'll have their drugs and weapons pretty well hidden. I'd rather sit back and watch them for a little while. If they don't know we're on them, they'll lead us to their stash soon enough."

"The Captain's not gonna like that," Vic observed. "One PP is breathing down his neck to close this one. We better make some arrests soon."

"Let me worry about the Captain," Webb said. "I want convictions, not arrests, and so does Holliday. Patience."

"I hate being patient," Vic growled.

"If Rolf can do it, so can you," Erin said.

Rolf, hearing his name, looked at Erin and wagged his tail.

"Okay, team," Webb said. "We've got three of us, and three goons to shadow. I'll take Maginty. Neshenko, you're on Burke. O'Reilly, you've got Newton. I'll give you each a plainclothes officer."

"When are they gonna toss us another detective?" Vic asked. "It's been months since Kira bailed on us. We could use another warm body in the office."

Webb shrugged. "I put in the request when she gave notice. It's bureaucracy. What can you do? You'll each have a mobile reserve standing by, two cars with two more officers each, in case you need them. Remember preschool? Buddy system. These guys are dangerous, so don't get too close and don't play hero."

Erin looked over Timothy Newton's information. He lived just two blocks over from Liam's place, in an apartment over a bar. He had no landline phone, unsurprisingly, and no internet connection. According to his parole officer's report, he lived alone. Then again, according to the report, he didn't associate with other felons and didn't have firearms in his possession, so Erin wasn't about to take anything for granted.

Her plainclothes buddy met her in the garage. Erin was startled to see that she recognized the other officer, a petite blonde woman.

"Piekarski!" she exclaimed.

The other woman grinned. "O'Reilly. How's it going?"

"What're you doing here?" Erin asked.

"Watching your ass, sounds like."

"No, I mean, what're you doing at the Eightball?" Piekarski worked for Precinct 5's Street Narcotics unit.

"Logan said you guys needed a hand with some street stuff. No one seems to know whether this is a Narcotics case, or Homicide, so it's all lumped in with Major Crimes now. He's rolling with your buddy, the big Russian. We just got here a couple minutes ago. We're gonna have to come up with some new ethnic stats, so we know who's buying the drinks when this is all over."

"Glad to have you," Erin said, shaking hands. Piekarski offered her hand to Rolf, who gave her a polite sniff.

"Let's see what they've got for us," Piekarski said, looking over the unmarked surveillance vehicle. "Sketchy POS?"

"Affirmative," Erin said. Their ride was a rusty brown van, no windows in back, that looked like it dated back to the early Nineties. Upon opening the back doors, they discovered it had a smell.

"Phew," Piekarski said, wrinkling her nose. "Smells like my grandma's house. She had a pipe burst in the basement and mold got into the drywall."

"Equipment looks good," Erin said. The van had the usual set of cameras and monitors, shotgun microphones, and fiber-optics. They ran through the checklist and made sure everything was accounted for.

"You want to drive?" Piekarski asked as Erin loaded Rolf into the back. The Shepherd gave Erin a very dubious look and circled several times before finding a patch of floor mat that was more or less acceptable and curling into a ball.

"I'd better," Erin said, handing the other woman Newton's file. "You can read up on the guy on the way over." She cranked the key. The van's engine was noisy, but it ran okay once it got going.

"So, we gonna bust his ass?" Piekarski asked as they drove up the ramp to the street.

"Not yet," Erin said. "We need to make the case. This isn't a buy-and-bust. We want to make a clean sweep, all the way up the chain."

"Too bad. There's no feeling quite like slapping the cuffs on a bad guy. Especially one of these big, macho bullshitters." Piekarski was about five foot four and weighed less than a hundred and twenty pounds, but Erin knew the Narcotics officer was tough as nails.

"Easy, girl," Erin said with a smile. "We'll get him."

"So it's my turn to see how your office does things," Piekarski said. "It's gonna be exciting, right?"

"It's going to be sitting for hours in a van that smells like your grandma's basement," Erin replied.

Piekarski made a pouty face. "I can see why you took the chance to hang out with us for that drug bust. We get better rides in SNEU."

They got to Newton's apartment and, by some miracle, found a parking space just a few spaces down the block. Erin parked the car. While she climbed in back and got the recording gear up and running, Piekarski took a walk and casually planted a mini-camera at the door to the apartment stairs. She disappeared around the building and came back a few minutes later.

"Got eyes on the fire escape and the back door," she reported.

Erin checked the feeds. All three cameras were working fine. "Okay, we're up," she said.

"Now we wait?" Piekarski asked.

"Now we wait."

*   *   *

Hours later, the sun had set, the streetlights were burning, and the two women were swapping stories of the most ridiculous arrests they'd made. They'd taken turns making trips to the bathroom, Erin had given Rolf a quick walk around the adjoining block, and Piekarski had grabbed sandwiches from a café up the street. Rolf was snoozing in the back.

Nothing had happened. There was no sign of Newton. Just after sundown, a street performer had taken up a post on the corner with a pair of guitar cases, popped one open, and started playing. He was actually pretty good, and looked to be taking in a decent amount of pocket change from the pedestrians. He was still there, the bar was open and doing a brisk business, and Erin was bored out of her mind.

Around ten o' clock, Piekarski suddenly stopped in the middle of one of her anecdotes. She sat up straight.

"There," she said.

Erin cracked her neck and groaned. "What?"

"That looks like our boy."

Piekarski was right. Newton was coming down the sidewalk. He was big and broad-shouldered, but there was a definite edginess to him. His eyes darted from side to side and he drummed his fingers against the legs of his jeans as he walked. The man looked seriously scared.

The two policewomen watched their target as he passed the guitar player. He gave the man a wide berth and a suspicious stare. A couple was on their way out of the bar, holding hands.

When they stepped onto the sidewalk, Newton jumped and shoved a hand into his coat pocket. Then he recovered and kept walking.

"He's carrying," Erin murmured.

"We can stop-and-frisk, bust him on the weapon charge," Piekarski suggested. A felon with a gun was a major parole violation.

"No. We wait." They needed more. A parole violation wouldn't be enough to get him to turn on his buddies.

Newton got to the door that led to the apartment stairs. He pulled out his keys and shuffled them around to find the right one.

The guitar player had put his guitar back in its case. He was kneeling on the concrete, opening the other case. Erin caught the motion as she was watching Newton. She saw the sudden, decisive movement.

"Gun!"

The word was out of her mouth before she'd consciously thought about it. Then she forgot about the surveillance mission. Even as she shouted and reached for the door handle with one hand and her Glock with the other, a dozen things happened at once.

The guitar player came up with a sawed-off shotgun in his hands, aimed at Newton. Erin flung open her door and lunged onto the street, drawing her pistol. Piekarski, with her good street instincts, whipped out her own sidearm and hurled herself out the passenger door of the van. Newton, twitchy as ever, saw the man aiming at him and turned sharply sideways. His keys tumbled out of his hand toward the ground and his right hand went into his coat again. The young woman of the couple gave a muffled cry of scared surprise. Her date saw what was happening and his eyes got wide.

"NYPD!" Erin shouted, but her yell was drowned out by the roar of the shotgun. Newton twisted and convulsed. A puff of white feathers blew out from his jacket and danced in the streetlight beam. As he went down, a blast of flame blew another hole in his coat just over the pocket. He'd fired through his own clothes. Erin didn't see where that bullet went.

Maybe three seconds had passed. Time seemed to move both very slowly and very fast. The young man on the sidewalk grabbed his girl and tackled her to the sidewalk, flattening her under himself. Somebody screamed. Erin had no idea who. The guitar player pumped the shotgun and fired again into Newton's body as the Irishman slumped against the brickwork and slid to the concrete. Newton's own gun fired two more times, probably in reflex. Erin shouted again and fired two quick shots at the guitar player. Piekarski was shooting too. Rolf, sealed in the back of the van, started barking.

The guitar player's head snapped around and he was looking right at Erin. She didn't think she'd hit him. The range was something over thirty yards, and between the dim light and the rush of adrenaline, she'd missed. She fired again just as he let go with another blast from his shotgun. She felt something sting the back of her knuckles, a hot, raw pain like a bad rope burn, and her hand jerked involuntarily. She'd missed again. There was an earsplitting crash from the van at her back. Then the guitar player spun and ducked back around the corner and out of sight.

"You hit?" Piekarski shouted.

"I'm good!" Erin yelled back. "Cover me!"

She sprinted across the street toward the scene of the shooting, grabbing some shelter behind a parked car. She could see Newton crumpled at the base of the wall, and the two bystanders lying flat. Rolf was still barking, but she couldn't take the time to let him out of the van.

Erin kept her eyes on the corner where the gunman had gone. She took a breath and ran toward the front of the bar. Then she crouched low at the corner and thrust herself around it, leading with the barrel of her Glock.

She saw taillights as a car roared away from the curb, but the small bulbs at the license plate were dark, probably deliberately deactivated. A horn blared and it sideswiped another car with a squeal of metal. Then it was around another corner and gone.

"Clear!" Erin shouted to Piekarski. "Call it in! Got a black sedan, Honda, southbound. Didn't catch the plates, but it's crunched in on the right door panels. And we need a bus, forthwith!"

"Copy!" Piekarski replied, jumping back into the van and grabbing the radio. Even as she did, a patrol car pulled up with lights and sirens going. A shooting in Manhattan pretty much guaranteed a very quick police response.

Erin held up her shield with one hand while she approached Newton, keeping her gun in the other hand. She saw a lot of blood on his coat. Little bits of the jacket's lining drifted down like snowflakes, sticking to the blood.

Newton's hand spasmed and he jerked it out of his pocket. He held a snub-nosed revolver.

"Shit! Gun!" Erin barked. She kicked out and caught the man's forearm just as he pulled the trigger. The revolver went off one more time, then spun out of his hand. Newton sagged and coughed. Blood spattered out of his mouth and nostrils.

"Clear," Erin said again, dropping to one knee beside the wounded man. He wasn't in good shape. He'd taken two shotgun shells at close range, both center mass; one in the chest, the other in the side. The blood he was coughing up meant he'd caught a pellet in the lungs or windpipe.

"First aid!" she shouted to one of the uniformed officers who'd jumped out of the patrol car. The man nodded and went back to the car. The other uniform went to check on the bystanders, who were cautiously sitting up.

The wounded gangster was staring up at Erin with oddly clear, bright eyes. He coughed again and spat blood.

"It's okay, Newton," Erin said. "Geez, they don't call you Twitchy for nothing. You nearly tagged me. Just stay still, we got an ambulance on the way. Stay awake, you hear me?"

"Shot... me," Newton said. His voice had a breathy bubbliness to it. He'd definitely taken a hit to the lungs.

"Yeah, he sure did," Erin said. "But you're going to be fine." She put pressure on the chest wound. The patrolman got there with the first aid kit and started pulling out bandages.

"Got... Liam," Newton mumbled. "Then they got... me. Gonna get... the others..."

"What others?" she asked. He was losing a lot of blood, leaking from more holes than she could possibly plug. The shotgun had punched buckshot through his chest in at least a half dozen places.

"Pat... Lonnie... the girl..."

"Girl?" Erin echoed. "What girl?"

But Newton's eyes had gone cloudy as he slipped into shock. He choked and gurgled and then went still.

The ambulance arrived less than five minutes after Piekarski called it in, which was better than average for New York City, but not fast enough for Timothy Newton. He was dead by the time the paramedics got there.

Chapter 12

"You're bleeding," Piekarski said quietly.

"Huh?" Erin was spattered with blood. She hadn't thought any of it was hers.

Piekarski pointed. Erin looked down and saw a red furrow down the back of her left hand.

"Oh," Erin said. "I think a pellet grazed me." Now she could feel the burning heat again and wondered how she could've forgotten it.

"Better have the medics patch you up."

The street was full of cops now. The EMTs, after determining Newton was beyond their help, were examining the bystanders. The girl had bloodied her nose when her boyfriend had tackled her, but they were otherwise fine. Unfortunately for the boy, his girl wasn't at all happy about what had happened. She seemed to think the gunfire was all his fault, that he'd somehow planned the whole thing just so he could deliberately smash her face into the concrete. She was listing his shortcomings as a boyfriend and lover, loudly and angrily. Erin wouldn't bet on that relationship's longevity.

One of the paramedics was only too glad to step away from the young woman and check Erin over. He disinfected the wound, pronounced it minor, and slapped a butterfly bandage on it. Piekarski didn't have a scratch on her. Then the detective and the SNEU cop sat down on the curb to wait for Lieutenant Webb and the CSU team to arrive.

"First time I've shot at anyone," Piekarski observed. "I missed, of course. Dammit."

"So did I," Erin said. She was mad at herself. The range hadn't been that long, the light hadn't been that bad, and she'd been in other gunfights.

"I've mixed it up with plenty of bad guys," Piekarski went on. "Fists, knives a couple of times, hell, even had one guy whack me with a steel chain with a padlock on it."

"Ouch."

"Yeah, I woke up halfway to the hospital. But never guns." Piekarski sighed. "You got any idea who the hell the shooter was?"

"Buddy of Diego Rojas," Erin said. She thought back, trying to see the guy's face. He'd definitely looked Latin American. "Colombian cartel gunman."

"You know he was out there?"

"No. I thought Rojas was the only guy gunning for McIntyre's boys."

"Think we'll catch him?"

"Yeah." They'd put out a BOLO for the getaway car, and this case was a high priority for the NYPD. There was a good chance a Patrol unit might grab him. But if they didn't get him before he ditched the car, Erin wasn't so sure. They didn't have a name, and the man had been wearing a bulky coat and hat. Erin thought she might recognize him if she saw him again, but couldn't give a good description.

"I should've hit him," Piekarski said.

"Me, too." Erin shrugged. "It's probably best not to get too upset about failing to kill someone. He's just muscle, anyway. It'd be nice to get the guys who sent him."

"Where are they?"

"Colombia, I'd expect."

Piekarski smiled suddenly. "You know, I'm feeling pretty weird right now. Wired. I feel like I want to get drunk, or maybe laid. You think that's normal after a gunfight?"

Erin returned the smile as well as she could. "There's nothing normal about being in a gunfight," she said. "Everyone reacts to it differently."

"You been in them before?"

"A couple times."

"Do you get used to it?"

"Not really. And you don't want to."

"Nothing personal, O'Reilly, but I think I'm gonna go back to SNEU after this. Gold shields are overrated. Too boring, then too exciting. You wanna come with me?"

Erin shook her head. "I like it here fine."

Vic's unmarked Taurus pulled up to the scene and squealed to a halt. The big Russian was out of the car almost before the engine died. Webb was still trying to pry himself out of the passenger seat when Vic ran up to the two women.

"Jesus, Erin," he said. "You gotta have all the fun without me?"

"You didn't both need to come," she said, getting to her feet. "Who's watching the other Irish?"

"I left Logan watching Burke with a couple of uniforms," he said. "We got the reserve team watching Maginty. You okay? Shit, you look like a mess."

"I'm fine. Just got grazed."

"You the cavalry?" Piekarski asked, looking him up and down.

"Some of it." Vic gave the blonde a quick smile.

"Another gunfight, O'Reilly?" Webb asked.

Erin sighed. "Yes, sir. If it's any consolation, I don't think we hit anybody."

The Lieutenant put his hands on his hips and took a look around. "So, that's another one down, two left."

"Three," she corrected.

"Oh, right, the guy out back," Webb said.

"And one of them is female," she said.

He raised an eyebrow. "Oh?"

"The last thing Newton said before he died was that the shooter was going to get the others. He said 'Pat, Lonnie, and the girl.'"

"What girl?" Vic asked.

"I guess one of the shooters was a woman."

"We lose one suspect and pick up another," Webb said.

"Some days, the best you can do is break even," Vic said. "So, who's this chick with you?"

"Chick?" Piekarski echoed.

"I call people all kinds of names, all day long," he said. "You gonna bust my balls about that one?"

"I dunno," Piekarski said. "Think I can find them, or are they too small?"

Vic grinned. "I like this girl."

"This is the first time a woman's been mentioned in connection with the restaurant job," Erin said. "We haven't got anyone on our radar, except..."

"Except Finneran," Webb finished. "You think it's her?"

"She's a trained assassin," Erin said. "I saw her make a headshot at better than thirty yards with a handgun last year. She's got the skills."

"And the contacts," Webb said. "And she's in town. But it's thin. If you'd gotten a name out of Newton, that might've been something, but as it is, we won't get a warrant. 'The girl' is just hearsay, and there's more than one girl connected to the O'Malleys."

Erin nodded, but she was thinking about Siobhan. The more she thought about it, the more sense it made. The Irishwoman had been brought into New York once before to do a hit. She'd left town immediately afterward. Now she'd come back, just in time for a major takedown of an O'Malley rival. Erin thought again of what her dad said about coincidences.

"Coincidence is like winning the lottery," she said quietly.

"Come again?" Webb asked.

She'd thought Ian Thompson was a good fit for the last gunman, and he was. Siobhan might be better. But they couldn't prove any of it. And there was something else.

"Sir," she said, "I don't see how Rojas is coordinating this. He's in the hospital, under guard, incommunicado. There's another gunman running around taking guys down. Where'd he come from?"

"Colombia," Piekarski said. "Right?"

"Right," Erin replied. "But how'd he know who to go after?"

"Easy," Vic said. "Rojas must've called him before he moved on McIntyre. The guy could've hopped a plane from Bogota this morning, got here in plenty of time to ghost Newton."

"I buy that," Erin said. "But how'd he know to track Newton?"

"Rojas knew about the other guys," Vic said.

"He only confirmed their faces when he saw the photo in Liam's apartment," Erin reminded him. "He might have recognized the guys on the street, but he'd have had no way to send the info to anyone else before that. We took him into custody right afterward. He didn't have a phone in the sewer with him. There's no way he sent the information to anyone else.

And even if he had, it was just faces. He didn't have names. This targeting was too precise, too quick."

"What are you saying?" Webb asked.

"I'm saying the Colombians have a source," Erin said. "Either in the O'Malleys, or in the NYPD."

All of them fell silent, thinking it over.

"Could be an O'Malley mole," Vic said finally.

"I hope so," Erin replied. The alternative was very unpleasant.

"In either case," Webb said, "we've got to assume this shooter has the other names, all of them. Even the girl's."

"We don't have the girl's name," Vic said.

"But the Department might not be the source he's using," Webb retorted. "The other thing we don't have is time. We don't know that there's only one Colombian in town. The cartel might've sent a whole hit squad. They could be making moves on our other subjects right now. If they think they can come up here and play Wild West, they're mistaken. Not in our city, not on our watch. I want a lid put on this, right now. I don't want any more killings, not even bad guys. Forget about spooking these guys. Get close, keep them alive while we build the case. They move, you move. One of them takes a piss, I want one of you helping him zip up afterward. Get going. I'll coordinate with CSU here, and I'll be right behind you as soon as I've put them to work."

"I guess the van's part of the crime scene," Erin said, glancing at the battered surveillance vehicle. It had caught the buckshot that had grazed her, its side panel resembling a colander. It was lucky Rolf hadn't been hit. "Mind if I ride with you, Vic?"

"Sure. You and the mutt both?"

"I'm not leaving him behind."

"What do you want me to do?" Piekarski asked.

"You want a ride?" Vic asked. "I'll get you where you want to go."

"We might need an extra pair of hands," Erin said. "Hop in."

* * *

"We going after Burke or Maginty?" Erin asked.

"Maginty," Vic said. "Logan seemed to know what he was doing. Burke should be fine."

"He does," Piekarski agreed. She was riding shotgun. Erin was in the back seat next to Rolf. "Is it always this exciting in Major Crimes?"

"I dunno," Vic said. "I'm asleep half the time, so I miss some stuff."

"What'd you do before you got this job?"

"ESU."

Piekarski whistled. "They have you knocking down doors?"

"Yeah," Erin said. "With his head. That thick skull goes right through reinforced steel."

"So I guess this must be boring by your standards," Piekarski went on.

"Any day I take fire is pretty damn exciting," Vic said.

"You hear about that thing in Little Odessa last year?" Erin asked Piekarski.

"Refresh my memory."

"Vic got bushwhacked by a bunch of Russian Mafia. There was a crazy shootout. He got tagged a couple times, but we got out of it okay. He was protecting a witness, this young Russian woman. He was a hero."

"Give it a rest, Erin," Vic said. "We got no white knights in this car. Hero, my ass."

"If she's not telling it right, you can give me the skinny," Piekarski said. "Maybe later, once we get off this babysitting detail."

"Babysitting?" Erin echoed. "I don't know what your teenage years were like, but when I was babysitting, we didn't usually get shot at."

Piekarski laughed. "You don't know the neighborhood I grew up in."

"Where'd Webb leave Maginty?" Erin asked.

"Just down the way," Vic said. "At a bar, of course."

"You saying something about the Irish and our leisure habits?"

"Every culture's got alcohol," he said, grinning. "C'mon, I'm Russian, for God's sake. The first thing a civilization learns how to do is get dead drunk."

"I'm pretty sure that's not true," Erin said.

The car's police radio crackled.

"Got a 10-13! This is Milton, shield three two six four! I'm at 17 John Street!"

"That's right around the corner," Vic said, startled. "That's right by the bar where Maginty was... shit."

Piekarski grabbed the radio handset. "This is Piekarski, responding. We're a block out, already en route."

Vic put on the sirens and sped up, using the horn to warn the New York traffic out of the way. A taxi tried to move to the side, but another taxi, oblivious, swung out from the curb directly into the first car's path. There was a crunch of metal. Vic, cursing, twisted the wheel. The Taurus squeaked by with a coat of paint to spare. He laid rubber at the corner, fishtailing and narrowly missing a panel truck. Then they were clear and rolling down John Street.

"We've got three people down, including my partner," Officer Milton was saying on the radio. His voice was oddly calm and detached. "And I've been hit. I need two buses, minimum, plus backup. One suspect, armed and dangerous. He's got a rifle, semi-automatic."

"Here we are," Vic said. "You ready?"

"Damn right," Erin said. From the sound of it, someone had just shot a couple of cops. She press-checked her Glock to make sure a round was chambered.

Piekarski nodded tightly, drawing her own sidearm. "Got your back, big guy."

Vic pulled up outside the bar, behind a squad car. The blue-and-white was parked curbside. Its flashers were dark. The car's windows were starred with bullet holes. Vic turned his car's spotlight beam on the passenger compartment. Erin slid out of the back seat, gun in one hand, Rolf's leash in the other. She could see two figures in the front seat of the squad car. Both of them were moving, she was glad to see.

"NYPD, coming up behind!" she shouted. Piekarski and Vic were right there with her, covering the street.

Someone was screaming inside the bar. It sounded like a young woman, probably hysterical. From the tone, Erin guessed the girl was freaked out but not injured. As the detectives moved closer, three people sprinted out the door of the bar, hands in the air, shouting "Don't shoot! Don't shoot!"

"Up against the wall!" Vic roared, covering them. "Now!" He didn't know who might be an enemy.

While he and Piekarski secured the doorway, Erin looked into the squad car. She saw two uniformed officers. One was working feverishly on the other with one hand, his other holding a Glock. The pistol was pointed toward the front of the bar. The man he was tending was writhing in pain.

Erin opened the passenger door. "Milton?" she called. She smelled gunpowder and saw spent brass on the floor.

"Yeah," the officer replied without turning.

"What've we got?" she asked.

"GSW, just over the shoulder," Milton said. "High-velocity round, went through the vest. He's conscious, but short of breath. I'm thinking pneumothorax." He meant a sucking chest wound.

The man under him gave a wheezy, rasping sort of scream.

"It's okay, Strucker," Milton said, still sounding unnaturally calm. "We got you. The bus is on the way."

"Where's the shooter?" Erin asked.

"Inside."

"He got hostages?"

"If he's alive, maybe. I'm pretty sure I hit him."

"How bad are you hit?"

"Not too bad. Caught one in the arm, high up. Bone's not broken. I'm fine."

Erin glanced up. Piekarski was talking to one of the bystanders who'd run out of the bar. Vic was pressed against the wall next to the building, aiming his pistol at the door.

"We'll handle the shooter," Erin promised. "You take care of your partner."

She and Rolf went around the squad car and met up with Piekarski.

"They say the shooter's still inside," Piekarski said. "He's holed up at a booth toward the back. They think he's hurt."

"Just one guy?"

"Just the one," she confirmed. "How you guys want to handle this?"

"We better go in," Erin said. "If there's still civilians inside."

Piekarski nodded. "Okay."

"Vic," Erin said.

"Yeah?"

"We're going in. One shooter, with a rifle, toward the back. I can't send Rolf, he won't know who to bite. You good to take point?"

"Copy that. We'll go on three. I want both you ladies right on my ass when I go in."

"I bet you say that to all the girls," Piekarski said with a tense smile.

Vic returned the smile. Then he was all business again. "One... two... three!"

The three officers rushed into the bar, guns ready. They passed shattered windows, broken glassware, and shaken, frightened people. The bar's patrons were huddled in corners or lying on the floor. No one seemed to be badly hurt. Several civilians pointed toward the back of the room.

Rolf lowered his snout and snuffled. Erin saw what he'd noticed.

"We got a blood trail," she said.

"I see it," Vic said. He moved quickly, not quite running, poised for action.

"Got a body here," Piekarski said, pointing toward the bar. A man lay sprawled there, unmoving, in a large pool of blood and spilled beer.

"That's not our shooter," Erin said. The man's hands were empty, one of them lacerated by the shards of a broken beer glass.

Piekarski knelt beside the man, feeling for a pulse. She looked up and shook her head.

They followed the blood trail further into the bar. At the back of the room, in the last booth, a foot protruded. It was clad in a brown dress shoe.

Vic pointed to the booth and cocked his head. Erin and Piekarski nodded. Erin gripped Rolf's leash tightly, ready to release him if necessary. The K-9, sensing her tension, was stiffly attentive.

Vic stepped sideways, pistol leveled. "Suspect down," he said quietly, but didn't move his gun away. For all they knew, the man might be faking.

He wasn't. Erin saw a slender, olive-skinned man slumped in the booth. A short-barreled automatic rifle lay on the table in front of him, one hand resting on the grip, but the fingers were limp. The front of his windbreaker was slick with blood. He'd been hit twice, low in his center mass.

Erin took hold of the rifle by the front grip and pulled it out of the man's unresisting grip. Then she took his pulse. Nothing.

"He's gone," she said.

"Good shooting by our boy Milton," Vic said.

"Erin," Piekarski said. She was looking at the dead man's face and clothes.

"I know," she said. It wasn't the same man who'd shot Newton. They had multiple gunmen on the loose.

Chapter 13

"We've got to get Burke in protective custody right now," Erin said.

Vic nodded. To no one's surprise, they'd identified one of the dead guys at the bar as Pat Maginty. They'd have to wait for Levine's report to know exactly how many times he'd been shot, but that was an academic question. He'd been hit repeatedly from behind, pretty much the same way Newton had gone down. Erin thought again about what her dad said about coincidence.

"I can call Logan," Piekarski suggested. "He can pick up Burke."

"Do it," Erin said.

While Piekarski called her sergeant, Erin and Vic helped the Patrol guys secure the scene. Milton's 10-13 had brought down all the available officers in the area, and the bar was swimming with blue uniforms. Milton himself was en route to the hospital, along with his partner. Both were likely to survive, thanks to Milton's quick first aid work.

While they waited for Webb, the detectives took initial statements from some of the bystanders. They'd already guessed most of what had happened. Maginty had been drinking Guinness at the bar. The gunman had walked in, taken a quick look around, walked up behind the Irishman, whipped out his rifle, and blasted him. Milton and his partner had been monitoring Maginty from just up the street. They'd gotten new instructions, passed from Webb through Dispatch, to move in on Maginty and keep him safe. Unfortunately, they'd only just pulled up to the bar when Maginty was killed. The gunman was on his way out, still holding the rifle, when he saw the cops. Both sides had jumped to the correct conclusion and they'd traded fire at very close range. Then the gunman had tumbled through the door, picked himself up, and dragged his bleeding body to the back, where he'd died.

"I've lost count of how many bodies have dropped on this damn case," Vic muttered.

"Fourteen," Erin said absently.

"Jesus. What do we do now?"

"Bring in Burke, like we're doing." Erin shook her head. "Lean on him, hard. Once he learns what's happened to his buddies, maybe he'll figure we're his best chance for survival."

Vic smiled sourly. "He can't give us much. By my count, he's just about out of accomplices."

"There's still the girl," Erin said.

"And the Colombian hit squad," Vic added. "That's what this is, right? Like those Russian bastards who tried to take me out in Brighton Beach last year. There's at least two of them, we've gotta figure on more. You know anything about how Colombian cartels operate?"

"Not really. I never worked Narcotics."

"Hey, maybe Piekarski knows," Vic said. "She's a Narc." He looked around, taking a minute to locate her. She was off the phone, so he waved her over.

"I talked to Logan," she reported. "He's got Burke."

"He still alive?" Vic asked.

"He was thirty seconds ago."

"That's no guarantee," he said grimly. "I got a twenty says there's a Colombian gunning for him as we speak."

"No way could they have locations on all these guys this fast," Piekarski objected. "Hell, the only reason we were able to scoop Burke up this quick is that our people were already watching him."

"Yeah," Erin said quietly. "They were."

Piekarski blinked. "You think there's a leak in the Department. You really think someone's feeding info to the cartel."

"You got a better idea?" Vic asked.

"I wish I did."

"It's got to be someone with access to our case info," Erin said. "That probably means someone in Major Crimes."

"Or Dispatch," Vic said. "They'd know where we sent our surveillance teams. I mean, we weren't doing this in secret or anything."

"Could be someone in Patrol," Piekarski added. "Or, hell, SNEU. There've got to be dozens of people who could've accessed this information. This is a big operation. Shit, it could even be Feds. FBI and Homeland Security are both involved."

"Homeland Security," Erin echoed. "Oh my God."

"What?" Vic asked.

"Agent Johnson. He was going to talk to Rojas at the hospital. What if he cut a deal, offered Rojas a chance at revenge?"

"He wouldn't sell out these guys," Vic said. "No way. That'd be murder for hire. Not even a Fed would pull that shit."

"Well, someone did," Erin said. "I think we need to talk to him."

"Not right away," Vic said. "We've got another crime scene to process. Those poor chumps at CSU are in for a long night. I bet they're not even close to done with the Newton hit, and then they've got to come down here."

"Sounds like you guys need to be about three places at once," Piekarski said. "Where do you need me?"

Erin was the ranking detective on scene, she realized uncomfortably. The other two were looking to her. She tried to think fast and straight.

"We need to talk to Burke as quick as possible," she decided. "And we need to keep tabs on Agent Johnson, in case he's our guy. And we need someone to stay on scene here until Webb gets here. Piekarski, can you hang here and talk to the Lieutenant?"

"Copy that."

"Okay, Vic, I want you to find out where Johnson is, what he's doing, and who he's talking to."

He stared at her. "Erin, you're asking me to run surveillance on a Federal agent."

"Nothing official. No phone taps. But we have to know what he's up to. Is that a problem?"

He smiled then, a nasty smile with no warmth in it. "No problem. What're you gonna be doing?"

"I'll talk to Burke. I assume he's on his way back to the Eightball?"

Piekarski nodded. "Logan and Firelli are bringing him in right now."

"Then that's where I'm going. Vic, you can take Rolf and me there. Johnson may be there, too. If he's not, maybe you can pick up his trail."

"Copy that. Let's do this."

*　　*　　*

In the Taurus, on the way back to the precinct, Erin got to ride up front this time. Rolf sat in the back, watching Erin attentively.

"Piekarski seems like good police," Vic commented.

"Yeah, she is," Erin said.

"How well you know her?"

"Not real well. I pulled a job with her squad a few weeks back. Drug bust."

"I didn't hear about that. It wasn't one of our cases, was it?"

Erin didn't want to talk about it, not with Vic, but it had bled through into their current case, so she wasn't sure how much choice she had. "I got a tip from one of my CIs," she said. "Liam McIntyre, if you can believe it. He saw a chance to take down a rival and tipped me off about a heroin shipment. I fed it to SNEU and they let me ride along."

"So she's paying you back now? Favor for a favor?"

"Something like that."

"You know if she's... you know, with anyone?"

Erin blinked. "Seriously, Vic? We've got more than a dozen bodies stacking up in the morgue, and *that's* what you're thinking about?"

"Hey!" he said defensively. "I just thought I got this vibe from her, like maybe she was into me a little."

"No, Vic, I don't know if Piekarski is sleeping with anyone right now," Erin said, rolling her eyes. "Maybe you should find out yourself, along with some other things. Like, maybe her first name?"

"Wow, look who's a prude all of a sudden," Vic said. "You must not be getting any yourself."

"You're amazing, Vic. I can see why they made you a detective. Absolutely nothing gets by you. My love life's an open book and you're reading every chapter."

"Sarcasm, O'Reilly?"

"From me? Never."

"Okay, I'm sorry I brought it up."

"Look, Vic, you're a grownup, more or less, and so is she. You do whatever the hell you want. Just try not to let it affect the case."

"I'm just saying I like working with her."

"And hey, at least this girl's not likely to try to have you whacked."

"That happened once. Once! Jesus, I'm the one who can't get away with anything around here."

*   *   *

Vic and Erin hurried into Precinct 8 and split up. Vic went looking for Homeland Security, while Erin grabbed Sergeant Malcolm at the front desk. Malcolm was a veteran of her father's generation, well past his twenty years but still hanging on. He smiled when he saw her.

"Hey, if it isn't Sean's girl," he said. "You got a kiss for a lonely old man?"

"Glad to," Erin said. "Come out from back there and bend over. Rolf, *küss*."

Rolf looked at Erin. She had, indeed, said the German word for "kiss," but that wasn't part of his training. He was waiting for her to give him a real command.

Malcolm laughed. "Looks like you've got a boyfriend on the Force already. Don't worry, big fella, I'll keep my distance."

"Say, Sarge, did a couple plainclothes officers bring in an Irish guy a little while ago?"

"Yeah. They just got here a couple minutes ahead of you, just booked him." Malcolm checked his log. "We've got one Leonard

Burke in lockup right now. I think the boys who brought him in are still in there with him."

"Great. Thanks."

"How's your old man these days? He miss the action?"

Erin paused on her way to the door. "Yeah. He was just telling me the other day how much he missed hosing vomit out of his car after hauling drunks downtown. He says a nice, quiet day on the lake with a fishing rod just doesn't give him the same thrill."

"You saying I should retire?"

"Might be worth thinking about."

Malcolm spread his hands around the lobby. "And leave all this behind?"

Three Patrol officers were trying to separate a pair of streetwalkers who were in the middle of a screaming match. A guy was standing a few feet away from Erin, staring past her with pupils dilated like dinner plates. He was having a conversation with somebody named Renny, who didn't appear to exist. Erin gave Malcolm a shrug and led Rolf away.

She found Sergeant Logan and his buddy Firelli in the process of figuring out the vending machine outside lockup. Firelli was feeding a crumpled-up dollar bill into the slot.

"Hey, guys," she called.

"O'Reilly," Logan said.

The machine spat the bill back out into Firelli's hand. He cursed and tried again.

"Where's my guy?" she asked.

"Room one," Logan said, jerking a thumb over his shoulder.

"He give you any trouble?"

"Nah. He tried to run when we showed our shields, but they always do that. Firelli grabbed him before he made it halfway to the door."

"Anything on him?"

Logan grinned. "Oh, yeah. Snub-nose .38, a switchblade, and a pocketful of nose candy. Unlicensed gun for a major parole violation, illegal knife, and Class D felony weight of heroin."

"It's the trifecta," Firelli agreed. He smiled. Then the machine gave him his dollar back again and the smile fell off his face. "You know how to get a bag of damn M&Ms out of this thing?"

Erin pulled out her wallet and handed him a less crumpled bill. "Try this one. So, we've got enough to hold him just based on that. He think it's a drug bust?"

"That'd be my guess," Logan said. "Say, what's going on? I heard some crazy shit on the radio, and then your CO told us to go in and snatch this guy."

"His whole crew's getting popped," she explained. "Two down so far tonight."

Logan whistled. "Gotcha. So, we're protecting this scumbag?"

"That's the idea."

"I assume we want something from him?"

"That's why I'm here."

"You want him alone, or you want Firelli or me with you?"

"Yes!" Firelli shouted.

Erin and Logan turned to look at him. He stooped and triumphantly plucked a bag of M&Ms out of the vending machine's dispenser.

"An addiction's an ugly thing to see," Logan said, shaking his head sadly.

"I'll talk to Burke solo," Erin said. "I've got some angles I can work. Can you guys hang around? If you can hold onto Rolf for a few minutes, I'd appreciate it."

"Sure thing," Logan said. "We'll watch from next door."

*   *   *

Lonnie Burke was a stringy, hollow-eyed guy who looked a lot older than the twenty-three years his file said he was. In spite of the cold March weather, he was wearing only cargo pants and a wife-beater that showed off a nice set of tattoos, including some prison ink. Logan and Firelli had snatched him from home and hadn't given him the chance to put on more clothes. Erin saw the edginess in his posture, the needle tracks on his arms. He was rubbing his elbows, either from the cold or from nerves.

"Hey, Lonnie," she said, taking a seat on the opposite side of the interrogation table. "You know who I am?"

He looked at her blankly for a second. Then she saw recognition in his eyes, followed by relief and a look of sly cunning.

"Yeah," he said. He leaned forward in his chair. "You're O'Reilly. It's covered, then?"

Erin realized he thought she was there at Carlyle's request. She had to swallow an angry denial. She needed Lonnie to talk, and if he thought she was on his side, so much the better. But she had to be careful. Word got around, both in prison and on the street, and if she screwed Lonnie too badly, Evan O'Malley would be sure to hear about it.

She hissed sharply through her teeth, warning him not to say anything explicit about her connection to the O'Malleys. "I'm working on helping you," she said, leaning toward him to match his posture. "Listen, Lonnie. You're in deep shit."

"Hey, it's just a weapons charge," he said. "And we can knock down the weight on the shit to a misdemeanor, right?"

"That's not what I'm talking about," she said. "The Colombians know about you. You heard what happened to Liam?"

"Yeah, I heard," he said. His face went a little paler. "Shit, that was the cartel?"

"Yeah," Erin said. "They know all about Liam's little double deal. They know you guys hit the restaurant, and they've got someone feeding them names. They've got guys right here, in town, right now, looking for you."

"How do you know that?" Lonnie asked.

"Twitchy and Maginty got whacked less than an hour ago."

"What? Both of them?" Lonnie hadn't looked good to begin with, and now he looked like warmed-over death. "You sure?"

"I just came from the Irish American," she said. "Maginty's there. He's done. They got Newton half an hour before that, outside his place."

Lonnie sat back. He didn't seem to be feeling the cold now. He wiped sweat off his forehead. "Hail Mary, full of grace," he muttered. Erin reflected that a Catholic upbringing left its mark, even on a guy like Burke.

"That's why my people picked you up," she said. "We had to get you off the street before you got nailed, too."

"Thanks," Lonnie said. "Hey, could I get a smoke or something?"

"Sorry, not here," she said. "Government building. You know how it is. Look, Lonnie, we're going to keep you safe here while we sort out these cartel goons. We can't have these out-of-town mooks coming in here and shooting up the place, right?"

"Yeah, I hear that," he said. "So I just gotta sit tight?"

"I need to get your last buddy somewhere safe," she said.

"Last buddy?" Lonnie echoed.

"Liam, Twitchy, and Pat are dead," she said, ticking them off on her fingers. Then she made her guess. "There's just you and Siobhan left."

And she knew she was right. She saw it in his eyes even before he spoke.

"Look, Miss O'Reilly, you ain't gotta worry about her," Lonnie said with surprising earnestness. "Those jerks find her, they're gonna wish they hadn't."

"I know she's good," Erin said. "But so are they."

"Good?" Burke repeated. "Lady, this broad... shit, we're playing Little League and she's starting for the Yankees, okay? You should've seen... damn. It was something else. You know what happened at the restaurant? You know what that was? Three shots. *Three*. Nobody's that good."

Erin nodded, feeling a thrill. This was exactly what she needed. Logan and Firelli were hearing every word, and recording it.

"You saw her do it?" Erin asked.

"Nah," he said. "Angle was wrong. But I heard. One, two, three. That fast."

"Okay," Erin said, pretending to be impressed. It wasn't hard to pretend. She'd seen the bodies behind the restaurant. It had been the best shooting she'd ever seen in twelve years with the NYPD. "Maybe you're right, and she can take care of herself. But you know how it is."

She leaned in again, speaking quietly, for Burke's ears alone. "She means a lot to Cars. Anything happens to her, he's going to go ballistic."

Burke nodded. "Gotcha. But I can't do nothing about that. I don't know where she is. She's getting out of town, I know that, but I don't know when or how. Hell, maybe she's gone already."

"What about the stuff?" Erin asked. "You got it stashed somewhere safe?"

"Yeah," he said. "What your boys didn't take off me. It's at a stash house downtown. Don't worry, nobody's gonna find it."

Erin couldn't ask for more information on that, not without risking herself. She was on thin ice already, and if a Narcotics squad swooped in on their drug stash now, she couldn't think of any way to square it.

"Okay," she said. "The word is, you sit tight for now. This is the safest place you can be. Just be patient. I'll figure out what's going down and get back to you."

"Okay," Burke said. "I'll wait."

*   *   *

"Who's Siobhan?" Logan asked.

"An O'Malley associate," Erin said. She collected Rolf's leash. The K-9 sniffed her hand and wagged his tail.

"You've got good contacts with these guys."

"Yeah," she said shortly. "Look, thanks for helping out, guys. But I need to bounce. We're on a clock."

"Sure thing, Detective." Logan smiled. "I guess we'll head back to the Five. Some of us have day jobs."

"You work nights," she reminded him. "And you belong to the Eightball tonight."

"Whatever. See you around, O'Reilly. But if you ever come by The Final Countdown, first round's on you."

Firelli grinned. "He's right, Detective. We got an Irish guy in lockup, so you're buying. We don't make the rules. That's Mickstat." He was referring to his squad's ethnic rule for providing end-of-shift drinks.

"Like hell you don't," she said. "But do me a favor, okay? Keep an eye on Burke."

"He's not going anywhere," Logan said.

"I don't mean watch him," she said. "I mean protect him."

"From what?" Firelli said. "We're in a police station!"

"Yeah," she said. "We are."

Logan gave her a hard, searching look. "You're serious."

She nodded.

"Firelli, you still got your chocolate?" he asked.

Firelli held up his half-empty bag.

"Okay," Logan said. "We'll hang here for a bit. Just do me a favor, and once this is over, explain it to me."

"I hope I can," she said.

Chapter 14

Erin ran upstairs to Major Crimes. Vic was at his computer, scowling at the screen. A few officers on loan from Patrol were talking things over by the whiteboard. She glanced at the clock. It was going on midnight. She tried to remember when her day had started and couldn't.

Vic looked up at her. "Hey," he said. "Get anything out of—"

She swiped a finger across her throat in a quick, sharp motion. He cut himself off midsentence, stood up, and walked over to her. "Break room?" he asked in an undertone.

"I need some coffee," she agreed.

They went into the break room, which contained a garage-sale dining table, a few beat-up chairs, a disreputable couch, and a very nice espresso machine. Erin poured a cup while Vic closed the door.

"Jesus, Erin, you're getting paranoid," he said. "You really think people are eavesdropping on us here?"

"I don't know," she said. "I just know we had surveillance teams following three guys tonight, and two of those guys are dead now. I don't want to broadcast the fact that we've got the third one downstairs."

"Is he safe?"

"Yeah. Logan and Firelli are watching him."

"Are *they* safe?"

"And you call *me* paranoid? Hell, I don't know. But if they're dirty, it doesn't make any sense. They're the only watchers who brought their guy in alive."

"That's a good point. Hey, could you get me a cup, too?"

Erin handed him the coffee and started pouring another.

"So," he said. "Did he talk?"

"Enough. The fourth shooter was Siobhan Finneran."

Vic smiled tightly. "Good work. I knew they gave you that gold shield for a reason. We got a location on her?"

"Not yet. He thinks she's skipping town."

"We'll put the word out to JFK and LaGuardia," he said. "And to the Port Authority."

"That's not enough," she said. "Siobhan's slick. She's gotten away before. We're going to miss her again, unless—"

"Unless what?"

"The O'Malleys will know," she said thoughtfully.

"Yeah," Vic said. "But they won't tell you."

"If they've got a leak, then her life's in danger," Erin said. "We're only guessing the Colombians are getting their intel from a police source. If they're getting it from an O'Malley, then they may already know where she is."

"Do we care?"

She gave him a look. "We're cops, Vic. It's our job to care."

"Even if they're hitmen? Hitwomen? Hitpeople?"

"Human life is human life, Vic. We don't get to put a different price tag on it just because we don't like her."

"Do you? Like her?"

"Hell, no. I hate her guts. And she hates mine. But that's not the point. She could be Adolf Hitler, I'd still try to bring her in alive."

"Hitler? Really?"

"Okay, maybe not Hitler. But anyone else."

"This is a moot point," he said. "Unless you can find her."

"I know," Erin sighed. "I've got one card I can play. But I don't want to play it."

He shrugged. "Then she walks. Or maybe catches a bullet."

"I know!" she said again, more sharply.

Vic held up a hand. "Okay, okay. Sheesh. Drink your coffee. You're less touchy when you're caffeinated."

"Did you find anything about Johnson?" she asked, changing the subject.

"He's staying at the Hilton by JFK."

"I arrested a guy there once."

"Without a court order, I can't access his phone records," Vic continued. "But I made a couple calls, talked to the hospital. He definitely talked to Rojas."

"Sean wasn't supposed to let him in before morning," Erin muttered angrily.

"They're Homeland Security, Erin. They get in places."

"Their whole job is keeping people out!"

"Anyway, it's possible Rojas could've given him a way to contact the cartel guys," Vic said. "No way to know for sure."

"Okay. Thanks for checking." Erin finished her coffee and started for the door.

"Where are you going?" he asked.

"To play that last card."

"You want me to come with you?"

"It's best if you don't."

"Okay. But tell your partner there, if you get capped on his watch, I'm gonna make him into a pair of mittens."

Rolf gave him a look that said he was welcome to try.

* * *

Erin sat in the driver's seat of her Charger, staring at her phone. She didn't want to do this. It was crossing a very definite line, and there was no going back from it. This might get the man she loved killed.

But they'd always known this might happen. It was the price they had to pay. And Erin O'Reilly had been brought up to make good on her debts. She dialed.

"Evening, darling," Carlyle said. She heard the background noise of the Barley Corner, the usual hubbub of sports TV and inebriated Irishmen. She also heard the tension she'd learned to recognize under his calm, pleasant voice. She wondered whether any of them had been truly relaxed in days.

"You heard about Twitchy and Maginty?" she asked.

"Aye. I've also heard your lads collected Lonnie Burke. He's still breathing, I trust?"

"Yeah, he's fine. I've got a couple guys I trust watching him. Look, can we go somewhere and talk?"

"I'd love to, darling, but I've a wee situation here."

"What sort of situation?" She tensed, imagining all the things that could go wrong in Carlyle's world. If he was able to answer the phone, she reasoned, it couldn't be all that bad.

"A couple of lads came in a short while ago. Out-of-towners, I'm thinking. I don't much like the looks of them."

Erin considered the sort of clientele Carlyle was accustomed to, and tried to imagine what kind of guys he'd find alarming. It wasn't a pretty mental picture.

"Are they doing anything?"

"At the moment, they're sitting down the far end of the bar, drinking cocktails. Tequila with ginger ale and bitters, unless I'm mistaken."

"Carlyle, I don't give a damn what they're drinking." She started the car. "I can be there in five minutes, maybe less."

"Don't do it, darling. If I've any eye for this business, they're watching and waiting for something. If they're startled, there's likely to be some unpleasantness."

"These guys, do they look South American?"

"Aye, they might well be."

Erin took a deep breath and plunged. "They're looking for Siobhan."

"You're certain of that?" His voice sharpened.

"Yeah. When did they show up?"

"Just a few minutes ago. Darling, why would they be seeking her out?"

She closed her eyes, the car still sitting in its parking space. "She was the shooter in back of the restaurant. She killed Conti and his bodyguards."

Carlyle was silent for a very long moment.

"Did you hear me?" she asked.

"Aye."

"Say something."

"What exactly do you want me to say, Erin? She's my daughter." There was real, genuine pain in his voice. But he didn't sound surprised by the revelation. On some level, Erin supposed, he'd known what Siobhan was for a long time.

"They're going to kill her," Erin said.

"No," Carlyle said with cold certainty. "They're not."

"Carlyle, stop," she said. "I know you've got guys who'll do this for you, but think, damn it! If Ian, or Corky, or you start blowing holes in people, then you go down, too. I can't protect you from that. Don't make me cuff Ian. Or you."

"Then I'm not precisely clear on my course of action."

"Oh, shit," Erin said, realizing the trap Carlyle was in. "Siobhan's there right now. At the Corner. Is she upstairs?"

He didn't say anything. He didn't have to.

"Okay," she said. "I'll have two dozen uniforms there inside two minutes. Sit tight. These guys won't try to fight the whole NYPD."

"You're certain of that?"

She wasn't. "There's just two of them," she said. "If we go in fast and hard, we can have them in custody before anyone gets hurt."

"Assuming the two at the bar are the only ones about," he said. "Who's to say they don't have a spotter on the street?"

Erin saw the situation. It was a weird kind of hostage setup. At least two gunmen, probably armed with sawed-off shotguns or automatic weapons, in a confined, crowded space. They were looking for a specific target, but she knew they were perfectly willing to shoot at cops. Two officers were already in the hospital, and it was only due to quick reactions and good luck they weren't in the morgue. Erin wasn't going to lose another officer. Not on her watch.

"Okay," she said, trying to think. "What if we just wait them out? They can't stay in the bar after closing time."

"I rather suspect they'll make their move before then," he said dryly. "I also suspect it's me they'll be going after in that case."

"Get out of there, damn it!"

"Easier said than done," he said with maddening coolness. "I'm avoiding eye contact with the lads, but I know they're watching me. Once I get up to leave, I've no idea what they'll do, but I doubt they'll allow me to simply walk out."

"Siobhan needs to leave," Erin said. "And they need to know she's gone, but she can't give them a shot at her."

"A grand strategy, Erin. I trust you've a plan to accomplish this?"

"I'm working on it. Look, even if you could kill these guys, which you can't, it won't make a difference. They'll just send more guys, and then they'll be looking for you along with her."

"I'm aware of the nature of the business I'm in," he said.

"The only way this ends is with her in custody," Erin said softly. "That's the only way we can protect her."

"Don't ask me to do that, Erin. Don't."

"I'm asking you to save her life. And yours. Plus the rest of your people at the bar."

"And how are you planning on squaring this with my employer?"

"Shit, I don't know. One thing at a time. Let's deal with the bad guys with guns first, okay?"

"I look around, I'm seeing nothing but bad lads, Erin."

"The worse guys, then. Think about it, Carlyle. If we take Siobhan in, she's got a chance. She'll get fair treatment and a fair trial. On the street, you know what her odds are better than I do. Let me help her."

"Don't pretend you're fond of her."

"No, I'm not," Erin admitted. "But I love you, and you love her. I'll protect her."

He was silent again, and she knew he was thinking fast and hard. Erin held her breath. She felt that her future with Carlyle hung on the moment. Either they'd find their way forward together, or they wouldn't. And he knew it, too. It wasn't fair for Erin to make him choose like this, but as her dad had told her more than once, life wasn't fair.

"If we're to do this," he said, "it's to be my way or not at all."

Erin let out her breath. "Okay," she said. "What's the plan?"

Chapter 15

It wasn't a great plan. In fact, Erin thought it was lousy. But what choice did they have? There was risk any way they turned. The worst of it was, she was still suspicious of the NYPD, so she didn't know if it was a good idea to call in heavy reinforcements.

She did call Webb.

"O'Reilly," he said. "Good to hear from you. I've been playing tag with you all night."

"And I've been chasing our bad guys," she said. "I've finally caught up with them. Where are you, sir?"

"At the Irish American Bar, cleaning up after the last round of mayhem. Where are you?"

"I'm at the Eightball, but not for long. I've got to go scoop up some Colombians, and take Siobhan Finneran back into custody."

"Why her?"

"She's the fourth shooter."

"Can you make it stick this time?"

"Sir, we may not have much time to discuss this. The cartel guys are after her, and they're going to make their move soon."

"ESU is on alert," Webb said. "I called them earlier, with all the shooting going on tonight. They've got the Apprehension Tactical Team standing by. Where are they going?"

"Can you have them deployed quietly? Without going through normal channels?"

There was a pause.

"O'Reilly, I can't make them do *anything* without going through channels," he said. "What did you find out?"

"Not enough. The more people we call, the more likely word gets to the cartel. Someone's on their team; I don't know who."

"How many bad guys?"

"At least two. Maybe more."

"Where?"

"The Barley Corner."

"Really." Webb's voice was flat, deadpan.

"Of course they are," she snapped, irritated. "They know Carlyle bailed Siobhan out. They figure he knows where she is."

"Where is she?"

"They figured right. She's there. So is Carlyle, and a hell of a lot of bystanders. If we go in heavy, there's going to be shooting."

"So we need ESU, but we need them at arm's length." Webb took a breath. "We need to take her outside. Okay, O'Reilly. I'll call the A-Team unit commander directly, bypass the Captain. Holliday will tear me a new one if this goes sideways, so I hope you know what the hell you're doing."

"I've talked to my source in the O'Malleys," she said. "Siobhan's going to go down the stairs and outside, fast. She knows guys are waiting for her at the bar. But they'll be moving her down the back hallway, no civilians in the way. There'll be an O'Malley car waiting for her on the street. We just need to be waiting outside. The Colombians will chase her. We can take them in the back alley, away from bystanders, hopefully with no shots fired. We grab Siobhan's car on the street before she gets away."

"Is Neshenko with you?"

"He's upstairs."

"Get him and your dog. Tac up, full kit. I'll meet you with the A-Team a block west of the Corner and coordinate. I don't know how long it'll take to move them, but it should be just a few minutes."

"Thanks, sir."

"Thank me in the morning, after we see how this plays out."

*   *   *

Erin still didn't like the plan. It was too loose. Too many things could go wrong. Carlyle might betray them, but she didn't think so. More likely, he'd make some modification to the plan on his own part. Or one of his guys would do something. Or the Colombians. Or Siobhan herself.

At least Vic was in a good mood. The prospect of working with his old ESU buddies always perked him up. He was actually whistling as he climbed into Erin's car.

"Glad someone's enjoying this," she said.

"Huh? Oh, I'm just looking forward to what I'm doing after the shift ends. Assuming this shift ever ends."

"Would this have anything to do with a blonde Street Narcotics cop, by any chance?"

"Maybe."

"That means yes."

"You're the big-shot Detective Second Grade, so I'll have to take your word for it."

"When did you even have the chance to set this up?"

"She called, while you were downstairs."

"Just do me a favor, Vic. Keep your mind in the game, so we all get to go home. Or wherever it is you're going. I don't imagine you'd take a girl back to your place."

"Erin, just where the hell do you think I live? I told you, it's a studio apartment. It's actually kind of nice."

"You said it was pretty much all man cave."

"Zofia likes manly stuff."

"Zofia?"

"You were right, I needed to learn her first name."

"Is that with an S, or a Z?"

"Z. I think it means 'wisdom' or something."

"You could use a little more wisdom in your life."

The Barley Corner wasn't far from Precinct 8. They reached the rendezvous point, a block away. The ESU Apprehension Tactical Team had just arrived. Erin liked driving her Charger because of its full-throated power and aggressive front profile, but the A-Team's ride made hers look tame. It was a Lenco BearCat, a wheeled armored vehicle that could take hits from a .50 caliber rifle and keep rolling. They'd pulled into an alley to avoid being too conspicuous while the team prepped for action.

Erin parked and joined the other cops. She, Vic, and Rolf had already donned their body armor. Vic gave a firm handshake and a one-armed hug to one of the ESU guys.

"Parker!" he said. "What've you been up to, man?"

"Oh, you know," Parker replied, feeding a clip into his AR-15, smacking the side of the gun, and chambering a round. "Same shit, different day."

Erin knew the Tactical Team was the busiest police unit in New York, probably in the country. They executed something like eight hundred operations each year. These guys kicked in doors every single day. This was just another job for them.

Webb stood off to one side. To Erin's surprise, she saw Piekarski there, too. Apparently she'd tagged along with Webb from the last crime scene. Erin glanced from the other woman to Vic, hoping to catch a sign of something, but both of them were in full professional mode and just nodded curtly to one another.

Vic climbed into the BearCat and came out with a tactical helmet, which he strapped on. "You want one?" he asked Erin.

"No, thanks. I'm not used to it; it'd mess up my field of vision."

"Suit yourself. A bullet in the face would mess it up more."

"I'm not planning on getting shot."

He smiled grimly. "No one ever is."

Erin did take a headset radio, however, and hooked up to the frequency the team would be using.

"All right, listen up, everyone," the ESU commander called. "As you know, some jackasses have been shooting up our city tonight. We're going to take them down. We've got a tip there's a couple of gunmen in the Barley Corner. That's the bar up the street."

"Floor plan?" Parker asked.

The commander shook his head. "According to Major Crimes," he said jerking a thumb Webb's direction, "we're not making entry. They're looking for a woman."

"Siobhan Finneran," Erin said.

"What's this woman look like?" another cop asked.

"A little taller than me, long red hair, drop-dead gorgeous," Erin said.

"I don't know about you, boys, but I just made plans for after work," he said.

"She's a contract killer for the Irish Mob," Erin said, wiping the smirk off the man's face. "She's an exceptionally good shot, and you should assume she's armed. She's killed three people this week that we know of."

"So who's our target? The gunmen, or the lady?" Parker asked.

"Both," Erin said. "Arrest everybody. And there may be more than two gunmen. It's possible they have guys outside."

"How will we know when the operation's on?" the commander asked.

"I have a CI inside," Erin said. "I'll get a text when Finneran's on the move. That'll give you a few seconds' warning. She'll be coming out the back door, into the alley."

"Okay," the commander said. "That alley has two exits. I want three guys at the north end. Parker, Hopper, Carnes, that's you. No one gets out that way. The rest of you are with me. We don't want this spilling into the street. I want a spotter across the street, under cover. Twig, that's you."

"Copy," said the smallest member of the team. "I'll hook around, get to the roof on the far side. I'll let you know when I'm in position." He jogged across the street and vanished from view.

"Once Twig gives us the call, we'll bring in the Cat and block the exit," the commander said.

"There'll be a vehicle there to pick Finneran up," Erin said.

The commander grinned. "Unless they're driving a tank, we'll get 'em out of the way. Then we'll have them all cold. Slap on the cuffs and we're done."

"We think they've got a lookout on the street," Erin said. "Won't they spook if they see this thing hanging out?"

"We'll be around the corner," the commander said. "Best we can do. I'm not risking the lives of my men if I don't have to."

Erin chewed her lip and nodded. All around her, men were loading weapons and tightening straps on their gear. She didn't feel like a cop in that moment. She felt like a soldier, getting ready to go to war. It wasn't a good feeling.

*   *   *

Then came the waiting. Erin had never served with an ESU tactical team. She'd kicked in her share of doors, sure. She'd been in gunfights. But she hadn't hung out in the back of a BearCat with a bunch of guys with assault rifles, dressed like dystopian Stormtroopers. She couldn't understand how they did it. She knew most tactical operations didn't end with people getting shot. But every bit of the operation felt military. It was enough to make her wonder if the world made any sense at all.

One of the guys, whose nametag said Madsen, passed around a pack of chewing gum. Erin gratefully took a stick. Her mouth was dry. Rolf, close by her side, was tuned in to her emotional state. His nose twitched ever so slightly, his ears were perked, and his muscles were as taut as high-voltage powerlines. A single word from her would make him explode into action.

And they waited. They waited a year, two years, ten maybe.

Erin checked the time. Ten minutes had passed.

"Yankees look good this year," one of the team commented.

"The Yankees always look good," Madsen replied sourly.

"Mads is a Mets fan," the first guy explained. "Someone's gotta be on the side of the losers."

"That's funny," Madsen said. "I talked to your wife last night. She told me the same thing."

Erin's phone buzzed. It was a text from an unknown number, probably yet another new burner from Carlyle. All it said was "Now."

"We're on!" she snapped, her voice cutting through the banter.

The ESU team was instantly all business. Dead silence fell. In that silence, she heard Twig's voice over her headset.

"Back door's open. Got a woman coming out. Long hair, looks like our target. Moving south. Got a car, stopping in front of the alley. Mercedes sedan, dark color, maybe gray."

"That's our cue," the commander said. "Execute."

The BearCat's 8-cylinder Power Stroke engine roared. The armored car leaped into motion, swinging around the corner. In the back, unable to see where they were going, Erin lurched sideways and grabbed for a handhold.

Then, without a single screech of the brakes or squeal of the tires, the ESU vehicle smashed into another car. The crash was earsplitting, the shockwave of impact running straight through the BearCat from front to back. Erin was pitched out of her seat into Vic, who sprawled against the guy next to him. Metal screamed. The BearCat kept rolling forward, slowly now.

"Go! Go! Go!" the ESU commander shouted.

Someone flung open the BearCat's back door. As the first two ESU guys dismounted, guns at their shoulders, shouting, Twig called out something else.

"Two bad guys coming out! Gun! Gun! Gun!"

Erin had no idea what was going on. She pulled herself upright and poured herself out the back of the vehicle onto the street. Vic was right behind her, Rolf at her side. Everyone was shouting at once. A car horn was jammed, bleating a pointless protest. She saw a cloud of steam gushing toward her from a ruptured radiator.

"Drop it! Hands in the air!" several officers yelled. Several others were repeating Twig's words. "Gun! Gun! Gun!"

Erin saw a dark gray Mercedes, its front end crumpled. She looked down the alley and saw a pair of men, pointing guns her direction. She hurled herself back behind the BearCat, hauling Rolf with her. She didn't see Siobhan. Maybe the Irishwoman had been sensible and hit the pavement.

Down the alley, one of the gunmen fired a wild burst. Bullets ricocheted off the BearCat's armored side, whining and skipping in all directions.

The response was immediate and devastating. Half a dozen ESU guys opened fire. Both gunmen went down. It was over in a matter of three seconds, maybe less.

"Clear!" one man shouted, and was echoed by two others.

"Where's the girl?" Madsen called.

Erin, acting on impulse, looked at the wrecked Mercedes. She saw the driver's side window was broken. That struck her as odd, but she couldn't think why until she remembered it had been intact when she'd first gotten out of the BearCat. Car windows didn't spontaneously shatter after an accident was over. She saw bits of safety glass strewn across the pavement in an outward fan. That meant it'd been broken from the inside.

"Vic!" she shouted. "On me!"

He was there at her back, holding his rifle. She, Rolf, and Vic moved in on the Mercedes, slow and careful.

"You! In the car!" Erin called. "Throw your weapon out the window!"

There was a pause. It was too dark to see into the Mercedes. Erin's skin crawled. There was a man with a gun inside the car. She knew it, but couldn't see him. He could be pointing it at her right now, through the windshield, and she wouldn't know until she saw the muzzle flash.

"You've got three seconds!" she shouted. "One!"

A small dark shape hit the pavement. It looked like an automatic pistol.

"Okay!" she said, moving closer and sidestepping toward the broken window. "Now open the door. Slowly!"

The driver's side door swung open. A few bits of glass jarred loose from the window frame and tinkled to the ground. In the alley, Erin heard the ESU guys securing the scene. She ignored them.

"Now get out of the car, hands in the air!"

Hands raised, Ian Thompson stepped out onto the asphalt. He was looking at Erin with a face of quiet calm. Erin, in spite of the adrenaline, felt a moment of whiplash relief.

"Turn around!" Vic shouted. "Hands against the car. Now!"

Erin realized she'd hesitated when she'd recognized Ian. She was embarrassed Vic had needed to pick up her slack.

Ian obeyed without question, laying his hands on the Mercedes. Vic stepped forward, slinging his rifle across his shoulder and taking out his cuffs. Erin kept covering Ian, out of habit more than anything, though he showed no signs of resisting.

Vic frisked him with quick, professional skill. He came up with a pair of spare magazines for a nine-millimeter pistol, along with a folding knife. Erin retrieved the gun from the pavement. It was a Beretta 92. She smelled the wisps of spent gunpowder that drifted from the barrel. It'd been fired within the past few moments.

"Shooting at cops?" Vic said, roughly pulling Ian away from the car by the shoulder and shoving him toward the BearCat. "Mistake, buddy. Big goddamn mistake."

Erin looked at the car window. Ian had been shooting out the side, not the front. He hadn't been firing at the BearCat. And it was the wrong window. The alley was on the passenger side of the car. He'd been shooting the opposite direction. What the hell had he been doing?

It was possible he'd been disoriented when the ESU vehicle had rammed him, and he'd just fired in a random direction. But she knew Ian. He was a veteran of two tours with the Marines, Iraq and Afghanistan. He'd been in dozens of firefights. He didn't panic, and he didn't shoot wildly.

She stood next to the Mercedes, crouched so her head was at the same height his had been, and pivoted, looking across the street.

It took a second to see the body lying between the parked cars on the opposite side of the street. All she saw was an arm, sprawled next to the hood of a Buick.

"Got another body!" she called, sprinting across the street. "Twig! You hear me?"

"Yeah, I copy," Twig said. "I don't see him, though. I'm on the roof right above you. The angle's bad. I didn't know anyone was there."

Erin and Rolf got there and found a man lying on his face. He was wearing a long coat and a stocking cap. A sawed-off shotgun lay next to one of his hands. Erin kicked the gun away and crouched beside him. She rolled him partway over. His eyes were open, but he wasn't seeing a thing. He'd been shot twice that she could see, a pair of holes neatly punched through the breast of his jacket. The holes were less than an inch apart, both straight into the man's heart.

"That's some good shooting," commented Madsen, coming up behind her.

"Yeah," Erin said. She'd been right about one thing. Ian was definitely an excellent shot.

"Who's this mope?" Madsen asked.

"I don't know," she said. "But he shot Twitchy Newton earlier this evening, and he shot at me." She flexed her bandaged knuckles.

"He dead?"

"Yeah. The other two?"

He nodded. "No sign of the girl, though. What's her name, Finneran?"

Erin stood up. "No sign? That's impossible."

He shrugged. "Got me. She was there, she hit the ground, then she was gone. I'm telling you, she's not there now."

Erin flexed Rolf's leash. "We'll see about that. Rolf, *komm!*"

They weren't done yet.

Chapter 16

Madsen was right. Siobhan wasn't in the alley. However, that was insane. She hadn't gone back inside the Barley Corner; the Colombians had been close behind her and would've shot her. ESU officers had been at both ends of the alley. There were a couple of other doors, which led to other buildings, but those were all locked, and the cops swore she hadn't gone through one of them.

Erin scanned the alley. It was clean and well-kept, especially compared to some back streets she'd seen. Besides the bodies of the two gunmen, she saw a couple of dumpsters and a manhole. Not many places to hide. Her eyes went back to the manhole lid as she remembered Rojas's hiding place.

"Tell me again," she said to Madsen. "You saw her, right?"

"Yeah. She was standing right there. Twig, you getting this?"

"Copy," said their spotter. "I saw her. Red hair and all, just like you said. She came out the back and started jogging toward the street, right at the car you wrecked. When you rammed the car, she dropped and rolled sideways, behind the trash bin. If she's not there, I got no idea where she is."

"She couldn't have gone into the sewer?" Erin asked.

"Not a chance," Twig said. "I'd have seen her. That lid stayed closed."

Erin checked it anyway. It was solid cast iron, heavy, and didn't look to have been moved recently. She took Rolf over to the dumpster in question. A woman could've hidden back there, but the other three ESU officers had already entered the alley from the far end and would certainly have seen her. All Erin saw was a basement window, at ankle height, with a wrought-iron grille over it.

"Check inside the dumpster?" Madsen suggested.

"It's not a real investigation until somebody wades through the trash," she agreed sourly.

They flipped the lid open. All they found was the rancid smell Erin expected from the trash behind a bar and restaurant, along with a few bags of garbage. Madsen poked gingerly among them with the barrel of his rifle, finding nothing.

"No," Erin said, denying the evidence of her own eyes. She pointed to the space behind the dumpster. "Rolf, *such!*"

The K-9 dutifully started sniffing around. Any dog on Earth would be delighted by the smells of half-rotted food, but Rolf was trained to ignore the more interesting odors and concentrate on human scent. Without a particular smell to trace, he went for the freshest one he could find. The sweat left by tense, excited humans had an especially strong odor, and he was good at picking it out.

He whined and scratched at the window grate.

Erin dropped to one knee beside him and tugged on the grate. It wouldn't budge.

"Here, let me try," Madsen said. He was six inches taller than Erin and much heavier, with a shaved head and enormous shoulders.

"Knock yourself out, caveman," she said. Macho posturing left Erin unimpressed. She didn't think this was a brute-force problem.

Madsen grabbed the bars and heaved, grunting with effort. He muttered a curse and tried again, with no result. He stood up and put his hands on his hips.

"This thing feels pretty solid to me," he said. "I swear, it's cemented into the brick. We could rig the winch on the Cat, but that'd tear a hole in the wall. Then the city would probably get sued."

Erin looked the grate over. It looked every bit as solid as Madsen said, but Rolf was insistent, and she trusted Rolf's nose more than her own eyes.

"Give me some space," she said. Madsen obediently sidestepped. Erin crouched down and ran her hands over the grate.

She was missing something. People didn't just evaporate into thin air. The grate was old and coated with rust. Hell, it'd probably been there for decades. The Barley Corner was an old building, at least a hundred years old.

Erin paused, remembering something Carlyle had mentioned. He'd told her the Corner's basement had been used as a speakeasy back in the Twenties, with secret passages. That way the bootleggers could smuggle their goods in and out, along with themselves if they ever got raided.

She felt it then, a metal lever hidden behind the grille, almost invisible. She squeezed. There was a metallic click. The whole window, frame, and grille swung inward on well-balanced hinges, revealing a low opening.

"Whoa," Madsen said.

Vic had finished loading Ian into the back of the BearCat and had come to see what Erin was up to. Piekarski was right behind him. He echoed Madsen.

"Whoa."

"Follow me," Erin said. She had to crouch low to get through the opening; it was less than three feet high. Rolf, tail wagging eagerly, hurried in alongside her. The other three were close on her heels.

Erin found herself in a dark storage room. She played her flashlight around the room. The place was made of brick, the floor concrete. Boxes were stacked against the walls, all of them bearing the labels of different brands of whiskey and beer. A single bare bulb hung from the ceiling with a string dangling from it. She pulled it and the room was flooded with light. Rolf was pulling against his leash, aiming for the one door that led out of the room. She let him lead the way.

For all the dozens of times she'd been in the pub, Erin had never seen the basement before. It really did feel like something right out of the Roaring Twenties. She saw all kinds of old bar furnishings: art deco stools and railings that'd been pulled out when the place had been remodeled; an ancient jukebox; crates of empty bottles; sheets of wood paneling. There was a musty, dusty smell in the air.

Rolf led the way through one room after another, taking no notice of the antiques. They passed several closed doors. The K-9 came to another door and scratched at it.

"Ready?" Erin asked.

"Ready," Vic said. His rifle was at his shoulder, ready for action.

She pulled the door open to find a staircase, leading up.

"Let's go," she said.

They went up the steps quickly, as quietly as possible. At the top, Erin put her hand on the knob. She glanced back. Vic, Madsen, and Piekarski nodded. Rolf snuffled at the door. He was sure his target had gone through it. Erin took a deep breath and yanked it open.

They spilled out onto the main floor of the Barley Corner, behind the bar. Erin was face to face with her friend Danny, the bartender. He stared at her, eyes wide. Erin looked around and saw dozens of patrons, all of them looking at the four cops and one K-9. The police officers were in full tactical gear, two of them wearing helmets, all of them in vests and with guns in their hands. There'd been a car crash right outside, followed by gunfire in the back alley. She wondered what these guys were thinking. Many of them were O'Malley associates, some probably armed, all of them visibly nervous. The worst of them had likely already skipped out the front door and the rest looked like they might stampede at the slightest provocation.

"NYPD," Vic said.

"No shit," said a man from somewhere in the crowd. "In case you forget, it says POLICE right there on your chest."

There was a ripple of tense laughter.

"Hey," another voice said. "Ain't that O'Reilly and her mutt?"

"Rolf, *such,*" Erin said quietly. There was nothing to do but keep going. The Shepherd went around the end of the bar and started across the room, sniffing busily. He was completely unaware of the social awkwardness of the moment. The crowd of Irishmen parted to let them pass.

As they went, she looked around for Carlyle. She saw him near the door, standing next to Caitlin Tierney, one of the Corner's waitresses. He looked outwardly calm, but his face was very pale. Corky Corcoran was next to his friend, hands in his pockets, watching the proceedings with a slight smile on his face.

Rolf led Erin straight to the front door. Carlyle nodded politely to them.

"Evening, officers," he said. "To what do I owe the pleasure of your company?"

"We're looking for a fugitive," she said. "Siobhan Finneran."

"Miss Finneran is not on these premises, I assure you," he said.

"Knock it off, wiseguy," Madsen snapped. "You're covering for her."

"Of course he is," Vic growled. "So don't waste time on him."

There were a dozen things Erin wanted, needed to discuss with Carlyle, but she could hardly do it here and now. Instead, she opened the front door and followed her dog out into the cold night air. She glanced to her right and saw the BearCat and the wrecked Mercedes. She also saw the flashing lights of several squad cars and an ambulance that had arrived on scene. Rolf snuffled his way around the corner, out of sight of the crash. He went to the curb, stopped, circled briefly, and looked up at her.

His meaning was clear. Siobhan had gotten in another car. She was gone.

"Son of a bitch," Erin said. She looked up and down the street, as if there was any chance of picking out a particular vehicle from the thousands of cars in Manhattan. It sounded like the only thing to say, so she said it again, the summation of this whole lousy case.

"Son of a bitch."

*   *   *

Nobody had seen anything, of course. Questions addressed to the Corner's patrons about a redheaded woman met with shrugs and mutters. When Vic pressed them, a couple of guys allowed that they might've seen a girl who looked kind of like that. She'd gone outside. When? A couple minutes ago. What car did she get into? Shrug. A taxi? Maybe.

Erin didn't even bother asking. She knew these guys, some of them personally, and knew they weren't going to give the cops a single thing they could use. She saw no point in embarrassing herself more than she already had.

"Okay," Vic said to Erin after his fruitless canvassing. "How many of these jokers are we arresting?"

"I guess the question is what we're arresting them for," she replied. "What's Webb think?"

"I haven't asked him," Vic said. Webb was still out back handling the latest scene, probably wishing he had two or three packs of cigarettes. "I think it's your call. Aiding and abetting?"

"Aiding and abetting whom?" she replied. "Siobhan wasn't a fugitive yet."

Vic sighed. "I'd really, really like to bust Cars Carlyle for something. I swear, that guy's suits must be made of Teflon. Everything just slides right off him."

"Maybe another day," Erin said diplomatically.

"At least we've got his boy, Thompson," Vic said more cheerfully. "It's not everyone commits a homicide right in front of ESU. He's going down."

Erin was silent. She wasn't at all sure of that.

"Can't we at least take Carlyle downtown for questioning?" Vic almost pleaded.

"I don't see how it'll help," she said. She wanted to talk to Carlyle, but not in front of other officers and not on the record. She gave Carlyle as hard a look as she dared, but he gave nothing away. He just stood there, tight-lipped and tense.

Webb came in the front door, accompanied by a pair of Patrol officers. He walked over to Erin and Vic.

"Any leads?" he asked.

Both of them shook their heads.

"We'll put out a BOLO," he said wearily. "Maybe we'll get lucky. CSU will get here when they can, but they're a little overbooked, as you may have heard. I've got uniforms on perimeter duty."

"Where's Thompson?" Vic asked.

"Cuffed in the back of the Cat," Webb said. "I figured we'd want to talk to him back at the precinct. I don't see any reason for the two of you to hang around here, if you want to take him in and see what he's willing to say."

"Sure thing," Vic said.

"Hey, can I hitch along?" Piekarski asked, coming over. "My ride's back at the station."

*   *   *

They booked Ian and took him into the interrogation room. He was calm and polite the entire time, taking everything in stride. He didn't lawyer up, but he also didn't talk. He'd retreated inside himself, to some quiet interior room in his mind. While he sat waiting, hands neatly folded, wrists cuffed, perfectly still, the detectives ran his information in the next room.

"His gun's legal," Erin announced.

"No way," Vic said.

"Yeah. Legitimate concealed carry permit. Serial number's on file, everything looks clean and aboveboard."

"I don't think I've ever seen that in all my years on the Job," Vic said. "Doesn't matter, though. He still shot a guy with it."

"Okay," Erin said. "Let's see what he's got to say about it."

"I'll watch," Piekarski said. "This should be good."

"Keep an eye on Rolf for me, would you?" Erin asked. It was better not to take a K-9 into an interrogation room.

"Sure thing." Piekarski scratched the K-9 between the ears.

Erin and Vic went in. Ian looked at them with a cool, calculating stare. Erin had the feeling he was gauging distances, trajectories, and potential threats. He was a young man, but a very experienced one, every inch a soldier.

"What's your name?" Erin asked, for the record

"Thompson, ma'am. Ian F." No smartass answer, no hint that they already knew each other.

"Age?"

"Twenty-six."

"Occupation?"

"Personal assistant and driver."

"To whom?"

He paused just a moment. "Mr. Carlyle, ma'am."

"What were you doing tonight?"

"I was asked to give someone a ride."

"Who?"

"A friend of Mr. Carlyle's."

"What's the name of this friend?" Vic interjected.

Ian cocked his head slightly. "I didn't ask, sir."

"Where were you taking her?" Erin asked, using the female pronoun deliberately.

"Airport, ma'am."

"Which airport?"

"JFK."

"What flight was she getting on?"

"I don't know, ma'am."

"Why'd you start popping off rounds?" Vic demanded.

Ian turned his attention back to the Russian. "I'd heard there might be trouble, sir. I wasn't able to get out of the way of the police vehicle. When my vehicle was disabled, the airbag deployed. I deflated it with my knife and assessed the situation. The police were containing the threat on my three. I saw a Tango on my nine, in the process of engaging the officers from a flanking position, so I engaged him. Range was about fifteen meters. I fired twice, neutralizing the threat."

Vic glanced at Erin. Neither of them had ever had an interrogation go quite this way before.

"You're saying you shot him because he was aiming at us?" Erin asked.

"At you, ma'am. You were in cover behind your vehicle, but open to the flank and rear. He was on your five, in your blind spot."

"Hold it," Vic said. "You claim you shot and killed a man to protect the NYPD?"

"To protect Detective O'Reilly, sir," Ian clarified, angling his head toward Erin.

"You know O'Reilly?" Vic asked.

"We've met previously, sir. In her professional capacity."

"You shoot a lot of people?"

"Not anymore, sir."

"Not since when?"

"Since my discharge."

"You shoot a lot of guys before then?"

Ian's face didn't change. In fact, it went completely rigid, as if it was carved out of stone. "Some."

"You like doing it?"

Ian didn't answer.

"I asked you a question, punk," Vic said.

Ian looked straight ahead, not making eye contact with Vic. "No opinion," he said. Erin considered how those words could express a very strong opinion, depending on the context.

"Who told you to take Finneran to the airport?" Vic demanded.

Ian didn't answer.

"Did Carlyle tell you to?"

Ian continued to stare at a point on the interrogation room wall. Except for a slight tightening of his jaw, he gave no sign he'd even heard.

Vic stood up and leaned forward, planting his hands on the table, putting himself right in Ian's face. "Look, asswipe, you may think you're some hotshot Marine. But you're not a soldier now. You're a goddamn civilian, in my city, and you don't get to go around blowing people away just because you feel like it. This isn't Iraq, you know that?"

Ian blinked slowly and looked at Vic as if noticing him for the first time. "No," he said quietly, "it's not Iraq."

"Your war hero bullshit doesn't carry any weight with me," Vic continued. "You got that? Here, now, you're just another asshole with a gun. You're going to prison, buddy."

Ian's face went still again.

Vic shook his head. "We're wasting our time," he said to Erin. "Numbnuts here doesn't know what's good for him." He went to the door and opened it.

After a second, Erin stood up and followed him.

*   *   *

"Vic, what the hell was that?" she snapped, turning on him the moment the interrogation room door closed.

"Huh?" Vic looked genuinely startled. "What're you talking about?"

"Were you trying to pick a fight with him?"

"Of course I was. I was trying to rattle his cage, shake him up. We do that all the time in interrogation, Erin. Sheesh. What's your problem?"

"The war hero thing isn't bullshit, Vic. You've read his file. It's the truth."

"So what? That doesn't mean he gets a pass to come back all screwed up in the head and murder people!"

"This wasn't murder!"

"He shot a man in downtown Manhattan!"

"A man who was gunning for cops! A man who was about to shoot me!"

"Says him!"

"I saw the gun, Vic! The same guy tried to kill me a couple hours ago!" Erin held up her bandaged hand. "That's how close he came!"

"I can't believe you're defending this guy! He's one of them!"

"He didn't commit a crime!"

They stared at each other. In the momentary pause, a woman carefully cleared her throat. The detectives turned to see Piekarski and Rolf peering around the door of the observation room. Rolf's head was cocked to the side, with his enormous Shepherd ears comically tilted.

"Uh... should I go somewhere else?" Piekarski asked.

"Nah, it's okay," Vic said. "Erin's right. Thompson's gonna walk. I just... Jesus, he shot a man! You think that's the only guy he's killed since he came home?"

"I don't know," Erin said quietly. "But we can't nail guys for what we think they might've done."

"It's been a long night," Piekarski said. "You two just need to blow off some steam. In my squad, Logan says everyone gets a freebie after a hard shift."

"What kind of freebie?" Vic asked.

"A do-over," she said. "For any one thing we do or say, as long as it's not illegal and doesn't get anyone hurt."

"Good policy," Vic said. "Look, I'm sorry, Erin. Guess I'm wound a little tight."

"It's okay," she said. "Me, too." She didn't add that Ian was the guy Vic should've been apologizing to, mainly because she figured Vic would rather break his own knuckles with a hammer than apologize to a suspect.

"What else we got to do here?" Vic asked.

"I'll process Thompson," she said. "You can take off."

"You sure? Webb may not want me running out right now."

"I'm in charge of the unit when Webb's not around," she said. "We've been on duty almost a full day. Get out of here. That's an order."

Vic smiled wearily. "Yes, ma'am."

Piekarski handed Rolf's leash to Erin. "See you later, Detective." Then she walked off with Vic.

Erin watched them go and rubbed Rolf's head. "Well, looks like someone's getting some tonight," she said. "You and I don't get to go home just yet. You good for a while, kiddo?"

Rolf wagged his tail. He could go as far as she asked him to.

Erin left the K-9 in the observation room for a moment and went back into the interrogation room. Ian was sitting exactly the way he'd been when she'd left. She pulled out her cuff key and unlocked his wrists.

"Sorry about that," she said quietly.

"No need, ma'am," he said. "We're all just doing our jobs."

"And thanks," Erin said. "Looks like you had my back. Somehow."

He looked at her without answering. Erin remembered something she'd heard once about veterans. If you looked in a man's eyes, they said, you could tell how much war he'd seen. In Ian's face, she saw a faint echo of all the combat he'd been in, all the bullets and blood and death. She wondered how he could possibly be so calm. Then she saw that he wasn't calm at all. That was just the surface he showed to the world. Underneath, he was always on duty, always ready to fight. Trauma psychologists called it hyperawareness. He couldn't help himself. That was how he'd managed, disoriented from a car crash, to maintain his situational awareness enough to see a gunman sneaking up from a direction no one expected. No wonder Carlyle called him the most dangerous man in New York City.

And she was turning him loose. Even stranger, it felt like the right decision.

"You're free to go," she said. "I apologize for the inconvenience."

He stood up. "Thank you, ma'am. Good night."

Chapter 17

Erin finally left Precinct 8 after taking care of as much of the case paperwork as she could stand. She drove home as the eastern horizon turned pink. She'd been working pretty much around the clock. There was time to grab a shower and maybe sleep a couple of hours before she'd need to be back at the precinct. Doctors and cops, she thought ruefully. Two occupations that couldn't afford to screw up, and they were the ones expected to run for days without sleep.

She made a mental note to ask her brother how much caffeine a person could take before it became dangerous. Then she realized how crazy that question was, and chalked it up to too much adrenaline and too little sleep. She parked her Charger and got out.

As she stepped out of her car in her apartment's garage, she saw a black Chevy Suburban SUV she didn't recognize. It was idling near the exit. Even as she looked at it, she saw a couple of men coming toward her out of the corner of her eye, out of the shadows from the opposite direction.

Erin was tired, but not too tired to recognize an ambush. She'd been bushwhacked in her garage once before, and had promised herself it would never happen again. Before she'd fully identified the situation, she'd unholstered her Glock and stepped back behind her car door, putting it between her and the two guys.

Then she recognized one of them and didn't feel any better. The lead guy was one of the largest men she'd ever seen. Mickey Connor, former heavyweight boxer, chief enforcer for Evan O'Malley, nearly three hundred pounds of sadistic muscle. The guy beside him looked like one of his heavies, a goon with no neck and enormous arms. Neither one had a weapon in hand, but that was no comfort. Carlyle had warned her that Mickey didn't need a weapon, didn't even bother to carry a gun most of the time.

"Come on, O'Reilly," Mickey said in his rough, gravelly Brooklyn street accent. "We're going for a ride."

He continued toward her. Erin gauged the distance. Ten yards. Seven was the magic number, the infamous "twenty-one foot rule." At that range, they taught cops, a man with a knife was an immediate deadly threat. She wondered how many bullets it'd take to put Mickey down. He was a bulky guy, and he might be wearing a vest. A head shot was chancy, but might be her best option.

"That's close enough, Mickey," she said, trying to put an edge of steel in her voice.

He halted. His lips curled into a hint of a mocking smile.

"Relax, O'Reilly. The boss wants to talk to you, that's all. Just talk."

"I'll bet," she said. Like hell she was getting in a car with Mickey Connor. She could think of safer, less painful ways to commit suicide.

"We already got your boyfriend," he said, pointing toward the Suburban. When she glanced involuntarily that direction, he took the opportunity to take another step toward her, moving with surprising grace for a man his size. His buddy had spread out a little, drifting to Erin's left.

"You ever been shot, Mick?" she asked.

"Couple times," he said. "Didn't take."

"You come one step closer, you're going to get shot again."

"I make you nervous?"

"Nah. I just don't like the way you smell."

She heard the click of a car door opening behind her and cursed inwardly. The O'Malleys had planned things well. She couldn't keep an eye on Mickey and his henchman while still covering her rear. But the two guys in front of her didn't have guns out. She closed her car door with one hand and used the rearview mirror on it to take a look behind.

Evan O'Malley was standing there, slim, well-dressed, impassive.

"That's enough, Mickey," Evan said. His voice was quiet, but it carried. "You're making Miss O'Reilly uncomfortable."

Mickey took a step back and folded his hands in front of his belt. His posture relaxed slightly, but Erin wasn't about to take her attention off him.

"I apologize if my men alarmed you, Miss O'Reilly," Evan said, walking toward her. "I fear they've given you the wrong impression. I only hoped for a few minutes' conversation with you, to clear up some potential misunderstandings. I simply thought my car would be a warm and comfortable place to have our discussion. However, if you'd be more at ease at another location, I'm at your disposal. We could step inside your home, perhaps?"

"Here's fine," Erin said. She liked the idea of Mickey and Evan in her apartment even less than having them in her garage.

Evan paused. "It's rather a public venue for discussion, don't you think? But if you're certain..."

"I'm okay with this," she said.

"Very well," he said. He raised his left hand and snapped his fingers. The front passenger door of the Suburban opened and Carlyle got out. He didn't look any the worse for wear, but Erin could see the strain on him. Another O'Malley guy climbed out of the back of the SUV behind Carlyle, an unspoken threat.

"Would you join us, Mr. Carlyle?" Evan said quietly. "We've just a few things to discuss, and then we can all be on our way."

Erin's pistol was still in her hand, resting against her leg. She knew exactly what was at stake here. This conversation would determine whether she, Carlyle, and Evan would all walk away from each other still breathing. Her life quite literally depended on what she said and did in the next few minutes.

And the gun wouldn't help her. She could shoot Evan, or Mickey, or even try to gun down all the O'Malley goons, but the odds weren't good, and even if she succeeded, it would only get her in more trouble. She slowly holstered her Glock and leaned against the door of her Charger, trying to appear relaxed.

"Okay, Mr. O'Malley," she said. "Let's talk."

Carlyle stood just to one side of Erin, on Evan's right. Mickey and his guy approached from the other side, but kept about five yards away. If they were trying to be unobtrusive and nonthreatening, they were failing.

"Several of my friends and associates have suffered recent misfortunes," Evan said. "A number of lads of my acquaintance are deceased. I'd be grateful if you would share your information on this matter, Miss O'Reilly."

Erin took a deep breath. Under normal circumstances, she wouldn't reveal case information to an organized-crime boss. But these circumstances weren't normal. She started talking, choosing her words carefully.

"My unit was called to a restaurant in Little Italy which had been the target of a hit. We discovered someone had shot up the place, then firebombed it, killing ten people: three restaurant workers, three representatives of a Colombian drug cartel, and four members of the Lucarelli family. At the time, we had no idea who'd done it. I now know the person behind the attack was Liam McIntyre. He wasn't there in person; we all knew Liam, and he wasn't a muscle guy."

"You got that right," Mickey grunted. His henchman snickered.

Evan turned his icy blue eyes on the two enforcers, who immediately shut up. Without a word, Evan returned his attention to Erin.

"Liam had learned Marco Conti, AKA Marco the Mouth, was making a heroin deal with Diego Rojas, a representative of a Colombian cartel," she went on. "Liam used three of his guys: Pat Maginty, Lonnie Burke, and Timothy Newton. He also employed an out-of-town shooter, Siobhan Finneran. It was a competent hit, not counting the collateral damage, but he made a serious mistake. Rojas's three guys were inside, but Rojas himself wasn't.

"It's funny," she added. "Most bosses don't like to drive themselves. But it saved Rojas's life. He hadn't gone in yet when the place got shot up. By the time he realized what was happening, his guys were dead, Irish gunmen were shooting up the place, it was on fire, and the NYPD was on scene. So he did the only sensible thing; he ran.

"Liam had screwed the deal, but that didn't get him anything. He wanted to do more than eliminate the competition. He wanted Rojas's drugs. So he contacted Rojas and let him know he'd be willing to take the drugs off his hands. It was a sloppy deal to offer; Rojas wasn't an idiot, and he figured Liam had been behind the attack. Rojas also knew his bosses back in Colombia weren't going to be happy.

"Rojas and Liam screwed each other. Rojas got a bead on Liam and started hunting him, but in the process, he got his drug shipment ripped off. Now he had no product. The only way he'd survive his own organization's revenge was if he took Liam down.

"I didn't know any of this at the time. Liam helped me with a tipoff earlier this year." Erin nodded to Mickey, who'd been present at that meeting. "So I figured he might know something about this situation. Carlyle set up a meeting for me. Unfortunately, Liam spooked, thinking I was after him, and ran out of the meet. Even more unfortunately, Rojas was waiting for him outside. We know how that came out."

Evan nodded, keeping his eyes on Erin. "So you went to Liam's flat," he prompted.

"That's where we found Rojas," Erin agreed. "He shot it out and ran, but we grabbed him. He's in custody." She hoped that was still true. "From him, I learned about the other members of Liam's squad. We started watching them, in case there was more trouble with the Colombians."

That was shading the truth a little, but Erin knew she had to look like she was looking out for the O'Malley family's interests. She was supposed to be Carlyle's contact in the NYPD. This was the delicate part.

"Rojas managed to get the word out to some of his guys," she went on. "We're pretty sure there were four of them. They made their move earlier tonight. We weren't quick enough to save Newton or Maginty, though we did get the guy who shot Maginty, but we got to Burke in time and put him in protective custody. He's fine. I didn't ask where he put the product; my job was to clear the homicide case. I talked to Carlyle about Siobhan, and he explained he had her safe for the moment."

"But a couple of Colombian lads were in my establishment," Carlyle said. "It was a delicate situation. I'd no desire to engage in gunplay in my pub, with so many innocent lads, and so many of our own people, hanging about. Erin and I agreed on a plan to remove the Colombians, and to safeguard Miss Finneran in the process."

Here was the lie everything else hinged on. If Erin told the truth, that she'd been intending to arrest Siobhan and charge her with multiple murders, that was it. She'd be lucky to survive. She had to tell it Carlyle's way, and make it convincing.

She looked at Carlyle and tried to seem pleased with herself. "We arranged for Siobhan to run out the back, knowing the Colombians would follow her. When they got into the alley, the back door locked behind them and they were trapped. There's an old hidden entrance to the Corner out back, from Prohibition days. Siobhan ducked through it as soon as my guys showed up. The Colombians tried to fight it out, and they got gunned down. The last Colombian was across the street, but Carlyle's guy took care of him."

"What's happened to my driver?" Carlyle asked.

"I processed his release a couple hours ago," she said. This was something else that would make her look useful to the O'Malleys. "He's probably either back at the Corner, or at home. He's fine. No charges."

Carlyle smiled a small but genuine smile. "That's grand news."

"Siobhan had plenty of time to slip back into the Corner through the basement," Erin concluded. "She walked right out the front door, hopped in a taxi, and got clean away. I don't know where she is now, but I assume she's getting out of town while the heat's on."

Evan considered Erin for a long, uncomfortable moment. She made herself meet his eyes, never an easy thing to do.

"So," he said at last. "What's to happen to Mr. Burke?"

"It's a tough situation," she said. "He said some stupid things in front of other cops. He basically admitted to being in on the hit. But he didn't say anything about any product, so there'll be no drug charges. I don't know what happened to Rojas's stuff; I suppose it just got lost in the shuffle. I don't know if he can get off at trial. He'll need one hell of a good lawyer."

Evan nodded. "Still, he's alive, and that's more than can be said for the other lads. You and yours took good care of those cartel lads. And I thank you for looking after Miss Finneran. You've answered my questions, Miss O'Reilly. I understand you've had a long and trying night. I'll leave you to your well-earned rest. Michael, Donald, Doyle, if you'll come with me."

Evan turned and walked back to his car. Mickey and the other two goons followed. Mickey gave Erin a last look. It held a number of complicated emotions. Erin saw disappointment, anger, suspicion, and a certain dark respect. Then the Suburban's engine rumbled to life and the O'Malley men were gone, except for Carlyle.

"Erin," he began.

She didn't even look at him. She opened the back of the Charger and got Rolf out. "Come on inside," she said over her shoulder. "I'm not done with you yet."

* * *

Carlyle was talking almost before they were inside her apartment.

"Evan picked me up on his way to see you. I'd no chance of warning you. He's angry, and looking for someone to blame. You did a grand job, turning him aside."

Erin turned on him. "Did you plan this whole thing?"

He stopped short. "What are you talking about?"

"Did you set me up? It's a simple question."

"Then it's deserving of a simple answer. No."

"You didn't tip off Siobhan?"

"I texted her a warning about the Colombians and told her to go out the back. That's all. Would you like to see my phone? The text history's in it."

"Then how did she know about the back way into the Corner?"

"This isn't the first time she's been here, Erin. She'd expressed an interest in the history of the place. I showed her around on her previous visit. To be honest, I'd forgotten she'd seen it. I'm a mite curious how you knew about it, though."

"Rolf."

Carlyle smiled thinly and gave a respectful nod to the K-9. "Of course. I should have guessed. Hidden doors don't fool a born tracker."

Rolf stared back at the Irishman and looked stern and proud of himself.

"But you let her walk right out the door," Erin said.

"Aye. What exactly was I supposed to do? You saw the lads in the place. Any number of them would have been proud to tell Evan precisely what happened. If I'd interfered with Siobhan, even if I'd wanted to, word would have gotten back to him. Then how do you think this morning's meeting would have gone?"

"You wanted her to get away."

"Of course I did! I've made no secret of it, Erin. But I betrayed her. For you, and for us. Are you asking me to go on doing it, over and over?"

To Erin's shock, she saw tears shining in his eyes. His self-control was entirely gone. Instinctively, her anger draining out of her, she went to him and took his hands in hers.

"And she knows it," he went on quietly. A tear overflowed his eye and spilled down his cheek. "I saw it in her face as she went past. She knew I knew about you and the other coppers.

I'll never forget the look she gave me. God, Erin, the worst thing an Irishman can be is a traitor to his own family."

"Carlyle," Erin said gently, "she's not your daughter."

"I've always thought of her as mine."

"But she knows she's not. She's been using you."

"Aye, that's what people do. They use one another. Even the ones they love. You used me tonight."

Erin felt her temper flare up, but the feeling subsided almost immediately. After all, he was right.

"Yeah," she said tiredly. "I guess so. Where's Siobhan now?"

"I've no idea. Gone from New York, I'd wager. Perhaps she'll be back someday, but I doubt she'll want to see me. I've lost her, Erin. She loved and trusted me, and I've lost her."

She put her arms around him and they held each other, wordlessly, taking what comfort they could from the contact.

"I thought I'd lost you, too," he added several moments later.

"Not yet," she said.

"I'm sorry, Erin."

"Me, too. This one hit pretty close to home. I thought Evan's guys were there to kill me."

"They might have been. It was a near thing. You've gotten good at this, darling."

"At what?"

"Dancing on the edge of the shadows, living on the edge of the Life."

"It's exhausting. How do you do it?"

"One day at a time. But you're right, darling."

"About what?"

"It's exhausting. You look like you've been through the wars."

"It's been a long day."

He put a hand to her cheek and brushed back a strand of hair that had escaped from her ponytail. "It has, at that. I've an idea, darling."

She smiled, a little shakily. "You've always got some sort of plan."

He shook his head. "I've a house on lease in the Hamptons. It's the off-season, but that merely means it won't be as crowded. Would you care to come away with me for a few days, get your mind off all this urban unpleasantness?"

"A vacation?"

"Aye."

She thought about it. "That's not a bad idea. I've got some days saved up. I'll need to clear it with my boss, of course."

"And I with mine. But it might do us good, aye?"

Erin looked at him. "How do you do it?" she asked again.

"I told you, a day at a time."

"That's not what I meant. How do you manage to be so..." Words failed her. She kissed him instead.

"If you're looking for answers, I'm not sure I'm the right lad for you," he said. "But we can certainly explore some of the more interesting questions together."

"Something's bothering me," she said.

"Only one thing? That's not so terrible."

"I thought I knew how the Colombians were getting information from us. But the guy I thought it was didn't know about Siobhan, not in time to send those guys to the bar. We've got at least one traitor, and I don't know who it is."

"Trust is a delicate thing," he said softly. "And you feel the lack once it's gone."

"I was telling you the truth," she said, looking him in the eye. "I do need to trust you. Don't let me down."

"I'll die before I betray you, Erin." It would've been a cliché if he hadn't so obviously meant it.

"I don't want you to die," she said. "Thank God we got away with it this time. What happens next time?"

"We'll take tomorrow as it comes," Carlyle said. "In the meantime, we've today to live. We'd best be about it. Look too far down the road, all you'll see is its end."

"And that doesn't bother you?"

"Life is the journey, not the destination."

"You're full of proverbs this morning."

"Near-death experiences make me philosophical."

"I'm too tired for philosophy," Erin said. "Right now, I'm going to take a shower and fall into bed. You should probably do the same."

"Is that an offer?"

"You're as bad as Corky sometimes. All I'm offering right now is hot water and a warm place to lie down."

"That's good enough for me. Given the choice, I'd not be anywhere else."

*   *   *

They shared Erin's shower, then curled into each other's arms. She'd told the truth; she was too tired to do more than fall asleep. But as she drifted off, she reflected how nice it was not to sleep alone. Rolf, sulking a little, curled up at the foot of the bed and glared at the man who'd taken his place of honor. He'd just have to get used to it, Erin thought. They all would.

Here's a sneak peek from Book 9: Flashback

Coming Fall 2020

They took 495 into Queens, passing Erin's old stomping grounds, then worked their way around north Brooklyn to the Williamsburg Bridge. That got them onto the Lower East Side. They'd long since caught up with the infamous New York traffic and slowed their pace accordingly. Erin considered how the increase in cars and tall buildings made her feel like the city was getting a hold on her again. She didn't care. Cut open one of her veins, she'd bleed one part NYPD blue blood, one part asphalt.

By chance, just as their wheels touched pavement in Manhattan, Erin's phone rang. She glanced down at it and saw Lieutenant Webb's name on the caller ID.

"He didn't waste any time," she said. She swiped the phone screen with her thumb. "O'Reilly."

"I hope I didn't catch you at a bad time, Detective," Webb said.

"Just on my way home, sir."

"Did you have a good few days off?"

"Yes, sir." She'd told him she was going up to the Hamptons, but had left out any mention of her host.

"Good. Break's over. I know you technically aren't back on duty until tomorrow morning, but we've got a hot one that just landed in our laps. You good to jump right back in?"

"With both feet, sir."

"Excellent. We've got a double homicide, probable home invasion on Warren Street. Apartment building. I'll text you the address. Looks like someone shot a husband and wife. We've got uniforms on scene."

"Okay. I'll be there as quick as I can."

"I'll be there, with Neshenko."

"Got it. O'Reilly out."

She hung up and glanced at Carlyle. "Sorry. Vacation is definitely over."

He smiled. "Oh, it's no trouble, darling. I'm glad of the time we've had. We'll do it again sometime."

"I'll switch cars," she said. She'd left her Charger at a parking garage a couple of blocks from the Barley Corner, just in case anyone was sniffing around her or Carlyle.

"Grand. Shall I call you later?"

"Better let me call you. I never know how long these things will run."

Erin pulled into the garage and parked alongside her beloved black Charger. She and Carlyle got out. He, always the gentleman, took her bags from the trunk of the Mercedes and handed them to her. She put her arms around him and gave him a quick kiss.

"Thanks again," she said.

"I love you, darling," he said.

"Love you, too." It was so natural and easy to say what had once been an earthshaking admission. Erin was amazed at how completely things could change. But then she was back in her old police rhythm, loading Rolf into his quick-release compartment, clipping her gold shield to her belt, and adjusting her Glock in its holster at her side. The Charger's 24-valve V6 roared to life and Erin O'Reilly went back to work.

* * *

Erin arrived on scene to the familiar sight of a pair of police cruisers and an ambulance on the street in front of the apartment. A uniformed officer at the door directed her to the fourth floor. She passed the paramedics on their way out, never a good sign. The door of Apartment 423 was open, voices spilling into the hall. A burnt smell, like overcooked steak, caught her nostrils. Rolf sniffed the air with interest. At least it didn't smell like charred human flesh. Erin had smelled that before, and would be fine if she never smelled it again.

She glanced at the door on the way in. Contrary to Hollywood, most burglars didn't bother learning how to pick locks. They just kicked in a door, or smashed their way in with a sledgehammer or crowbar. This door showed no signs of damage. The lock and doorknob were intact.

On her left was a small closet, everything hanging neatly in place. She saw coats, scarves, boots, and shoes lined up in tidy rows. On her right was the kitchen. Wisps of smoke trailed around the edges of the oven door. The smoke alarm was sitting on the counter, deactivated, batteries next to it. Food and utensils were scattered haphazardly, like someone had been interrupted in the middle of making dinner. A broad-bladed knife lay on the cutting board with some carrots half chopped.

Erin kept going, following the voices. She pulled on a pair of disposable gloves from the roll she kept in her car. She came around the kitchen doorway and into the combination dining room/living room.

"There she is," Vic Neshenko said. "Welcome to the party." He, Lieutenant Webb, and Doctor Sarah Levine, the Medical Examiner, were standing around a pair of bodies. The carpet was beige. Blood had pooled under the corpses, a dark maroon.

"Some party," Erin said. She saw a string of balloons that hung across the room with a "WELCOME HOME" banner in the middle. A sheet cake, like you'd buy at a grocery store, sat on the coffee table. Several liquor bottles surrounded the cake, accompanied by a package of red plastic cups. One of the bottles had spilled on the floor, making another dark stain on the carpet.

"We've got preliminary ID on the victims," Webb said. "Husband and wife, Frank and Helen Carson."

"The doc's been here a few minutes," Vic said. "Whaddaya say, Doc? What killed these two?"

Levine had been making some notes and hadn't acknowledged Erin's presence at all. She looked up at Vic with mild annoyance, like he was interrupting her in the middle of something more interesting.

"Both victims suffered multiple gunshot wounds," she said. "Preliminary forensics indicate a large-caliber handgun, probably .45 caliber. It appears the male victim was struck first. As you can see, he was probably facing his shooter and fell on his back. From the angle of the bodies, the female victim was not standing when she was shot. I believe she was kneeling beside the male victim. She then fell forward across him. Death was instantaneous in both cases. The female was struck by three bullets, two in the torso, one in the cranium. The torso wounds would likely have proved fatal, as one transects the aorta and the other appears to have perforated the right lung. However, that is academic, as the third bullet destroyed the cranium. As you can see, the entrance wound is just above the right eye. The exit wound detached most of the back of the skull. Cause of death was destruction of the brain."

"Yeah, that'll do it," Vic muttered. "I've seen .45 slugs before. They do some damage."

Erin tried to retreat into the clinical detachment cops and doctors learned as a coping mechanism. She told herself these bodies weren't people anymore. They were just the shells people left behind when they died, shells the detectives could use to find out who'd killed them and why.

Levine was still talking. "I haven't been able to make a full examination of either body, due to their entangled posture, but I believe the male was also struck at least once in the torso, as well as a single bullet to the cranium. Cause of death is congruent with the other victim, with similar wound presentation."

"Brass?" Erin asked Vic.

He nodded and pointed to the hallway that led to the bathroom and bedroom. Little yellow plastic markers with black numbers had been placed beside each shell casing. Erin counted six.

"That's a little weird," she said.

"Just means it was an automatic, not a revolver," Vic said with a shrug. "Both can be chambered in .45 caliber."

"I mean the location," she said. "It looks like the killer didn't come in through the front door."

"Right," Webb said. "He didn't come in through the kitchen. They would've seen him. It looks like he came from either the bathroom or the bedroom."

Erin walked carefully around the shell casings. Rolf sniffed at them, catching the familiar scent of gunpowder, and padded alongside her. The bathroom door was ajar. She poked it open the rest of the way. Like the rest of the apartment, there was no sign of robbery or ransacking. She caught a faint, sour smell that reminded her of dirty subway stations, or the back of her cruiser after a night of transporting drunks. The window was small and unopened. She went to it and peered through. She saw the street four floors down.

She came back into the hallway and, together with Rolf, tried the bedroom. The bed was neatly made. Very neatly, in fact. The corners were perfectly squared, the sheet stretched so tight she figured she could bounce a quarter off it. The bedroom window also overlooked the street in front of the building.

"No fire escape," she reported, coming back to the living room. "And no sign of entry through either window. They latch from the inside. I don't think anyone could've climbed in."

"So we can rule out Spider-man," Vic said. "But I guess he could be a ninja."

"A ninja," Webb said, deadpan.

"Sure!" Vic said defensively. "You know, an assassin, in those black suits. He sneaks in while the couple's getting ready for their party..."

"Ninjas don't use .45s," Erin said.

"*That's* your problem with this theory?" Webb asked, raising an eyebrow.

"That was the first one I thought of," she said.

"Okay, probably not a ninja," Webb said. "What I want to know is, who else was supposed to be here?"

"For the party?" Erin asked.

"Yeah," Vic said. "Who was being welcomed home? And what about the rest of the guests?"

"Let's start by finding out who the Carsons were," Webb said. "We're just guessing this is who the victims are, since it's their apartment. Facial recognition... well, that's not going to be much help here. Levine, check them for ID. I want a positive identification as quickly as possible. Then let's find out whether one of them was coming home, or if this cake was for someone else."

Erin was looking at the cake. Someone had decorated it with the words, "Welcome Back, Hero!" Beneath that was an American flag made of frosting, and little starbursts that might be intended to be fireworks.

"Hero," she said quietly. "I think maybe this party was for a soldier."

"Looks like a war followed our boy home," Vic said.

Ready for more?

Join Steven Henry's author email list
for the latest on new releases, upcoming books and
series, behind-the-scenes details, events, and more.

Be the first to know about new releases in the Erin
O'Reilly Mysteries by signing up at
tinyurl.com/StevenHenryEmail

About the Author

Steven Henry learned how to read almost before he learned how to walk. Ever since he began reading stories, he wanted to put his own on the page. He lives a very quiet and ordinary life in Minnesota with his wife and dog.

Also by Steven Henry

Ember of Dreams
The Clarion Chronicles, Book One

When magic awakens a long-forgotten folk, a noble lady, a young apprentice, and a solitary blacksmith band together to prevent war and seek understanding between humans and elves.

Lady Kristyn Tremayne – An otherwise unremarkable young lady's open heart and inquisitive mind reveal a hidden world of magic.

Robert Blackford – A humble harp maker's apprentice dreams of being a hero.

Master Gabriel Zane – A master blacksmith's pursuit of perfection leads him to craft an enchanted sword, drawing him out of his isolation and far from his cozy home.

Lord Luthor Carnarvon – A lonely nobleman with a dark past has won the heart of Kristyn's mother, but at what cost?

Readers love *Ember of Dreams*

"The more I got to know the characters, the more I liked them. The female lead in particular is a treat to accompany on her journey from ordinary to extraordinary."

"The author's deep understanding of his protagonists' motivations and keen eye for psychological detail make Robert and his companions a likable and memorable cast."

Learn more at tinyurl.com/emberofdreams.

More great titles from Clickworks Press

www.clickworkspress.com

The Altered Wake
Megan Morgan

Amid growing unrest, a family secret and an ancient laboratory unleash long-hidden superhuman abilities. Now newly-promoted Sentinel Cameron Kardell must chase down a rogue superhuman who holds the key to the powers' origin: the greatest threat Cotarion has seen in centuries – and Cam's best friend.

"Incredible. Starts out gripping and keeps getting better."

Learn more at clickworkspress.com/sentinel1.

Hubris Towers: The Complete First Season
Ben Y. Faroe & Bill Hoard

Comedy of manners meets comedy of errors in a new series for fans of Fawlty Towers and P. G. Wodehouse.

"So funny and endearing"

"Had me laughing so hard that I had to put it down to catch my breath"

"Astoundingly, outrageously funny!"

Learn more at clickworkspress.com/hts01.

Death's Dream Kingdom
Gabriel Blanchard

A young woman of Victorian London has been transformed into a vampire. Can she survive the world of the immortal dead— or perhaps, escape it?

"The wit and humor are as Victorian as the setting... a winsomely vulnerable and tremendously crafted work of art."

"A dramatic, engaging novel which explores themes of death, love, damnation, and redemption."

Learn more at clickworkspress.com/ddk.

Share the love!

Join our microlending team at
kiva.org/team/clickworkspress.

Keep in touch!

Join the Clickworks Press email list
and get freebies, production updates, special deals,
behind-the-scenes sneak peeks, and more.

Sign up today at clickworkspress.com/join.

CPSIA information can be obtained
at www.ICGtesting.com
Printed in the USA
BVHW041229130222
628599BV00007BA/116/J

9 781943 383665